Bjørnstjerne Bjørnson

Ovind

A Story Of Country Life In Norway

Bjørnstjerne Bjørnson

Ovind

A Story Of Country Life In Norway

ISBN/EAN: 9783742813916

Manufactured in Europe, USA, Canada, Australia, Japa

Cover: Foto ©Andreas Hilbeck / pixelio.de

Manufactured and distributed by brebook publishing software
(www.brebook.com)

Bjørnstjerne Bjørnson

Ovind

O V I N D:

A Story of Country Life in Norway,

BY

BJÖRNSTJERNE BJÖRNSON.

TRANSLATED FROM THE NORWEGIAN
"EN GLAD GUT,"

BY

SIVERT AND ELIZABETH HJERLEID.

LONDON : SIMPKIN, MARSHALL, AND CO.
MIDDLESBROUGH : BURNETT AND HOOD.

—

1869.

TRANSLATORS' PREFACE.

In offering to the public our Translation of Ovind, we wish to say that the work was commenced simply for the pleasure of it, and without any view to publication; but having completed it, we have decided to follow the advice of many of our friends who have read the book, and who think it a pity to keep in manuscript the translation of a work so original as this. It is therefore offered to the English reader, in the hope that it will meet with the same success in this country that it has done in others; for BJÖRNSTJERNE BJÖRNSON, that singular man who seemed so long destined to be distinguished for naught but foolish pranks as a boy, and inaptitude at school and college, has won for himself high literary honors, not only in his native land but throughout Northern Europe. A restless nature, wandering in a wilderness of unfixed purpose, he has repeatedly been on the point of giving himself up as good for naught, until at last the sequestered valley, and the lowly and quiet life of his home, broke upon his wondering eye, in forms he had been seeking in that dreamy half-conscious instinct, which has so often been the harbinger of greatness. . .

The " Bonde," that sturdy aristocrat of a northern settlement, a man of noble descent, a lord of his ground, and the mainstay of his country, covering under the rugged garb of his matter-of-fact life, a heart that beats warm with attachment to his fellow man, and an inborn pride, nurtured by Saga memories and family traditions,—is BJÖRNSON'S text, and a text he handles well. His romances are true to nature, and the sombre grandeur of his land inspires him with ideas which we meet with only in his writings, and which are completely his own. There is a weird light over his whole mind, reflected in his works, which does not repel, but allures. In short, BJÖRNSON, of all men living, seems to have entered most entirely into the life of his nation as it is in its reality, the life which exists on the national traditions, customs, thought, handed down from generation to generation.

The story, which it has been our endeavour to translate as literally as possible, is one of the author's earliest works. In the original the chapters are without headings, but we have added them as more consonant with English taste and custom. As the Norwegian title, " En glad Gut," scarcely bears translation, we have given the name of the hero of the story to the book. Thinking it would be acceptable to our readers, we have added two of BJÖRN-SON's shorter pieces, "The Eagle's Nest," and " The Father." .

We should not feel to be doing HERR BJÖRNSON justice, if we spoke only of his romances, and omitted to mention his success as a poet and dramatist. In the drama he has mostly chosen for his subjects, scenes in old Norwegian history, but his play entitled, "Mary Stuart," and another of more general interest, "The newly-married couple," would perhaps be better suited to the English reader.

NORTH ORMESBY,
    MIDDLESBROUGH, OCTOBER, 1869.

CONTENTS.

OVIND.

CHAP. I.

THE LOST GOAT.

THEY called him Ovind, and he cried when he was born. But when he could sit upon his mother's lap he smiled, and when they lit the candle in the dusk, he laughed and laughed again, but cried when he couldn't come to it.

" This child will be something rare," said the mother.

There, where he was born, the wild rocks overhung. From the top of the ridge, the firs and birch looked down upon the cottage ; the bird cherry strewed its flowers on the roof. And up on the roof grazed Ovind's little goat ;

they kept him there that he mightn't stray, and
Ovind gathered leaves and grass for him. One
fine morning the goat leapt down, and skipped
among the rocks, away where he had never
been before. When Ovind came out in the
afternoon, the goat was gone. He thought at
once of a fox, and grew hot and listened—" Billy,
Billy, Billy, Bil-ly goat!" "Ba-a-a!" he answered
up from the ridge, laid his head to one side, and
looked down.

By the side of the goat sat a little girl. " Is
the goat yours ?" said she.

Ovind stood with open eyes and mouth, and
stuck both his hands in his pocket. " Who are
you ?" said he.

" I am Marit, my mother's pet, my father's
darling, the fairy in the house, granddaughter
to Ole Nordistuen at Heidegaard, four years
old in Autumn, two days after the frosty
nights !"

" Oh ! are you that !" said he, as he drew a

long breath, for he had not stirred while she
spoke.

" Is the goat yours ?" said the little girl
again.

" Why, yes," said he, and looked up.

" I have taken such a fancy to this goat ;—
you won't give it to me ?"

" No, that I won't."

She twisted herself, looked down upon him,
and said : " But if I give you a butter biscuit,
can I get the goat ?"

Ovind was of poor folk, he had only eaten
butter biscuit once in his life, that was when his
grandfather came, and the like he had never
tasted before or since. "Let me first see the
biscuit," said he.

She held up a large one—" Here it is !"—and
tossed it down.

" Oh ! it's broken !" said the boy, and he
carefully gathered up every crumb ;—the smallest bit he must taste, and it was so good that

he must take just another, and another, till
before he knew it, the whole biscuit was
gone.

" Now the goat is mine," said the little girl.

The boy stopped with the last bit in his
mouth. The girl sat and smiled, the goat
standing by her side, with his white breast and
dark brown shaggy hair.

" Couldn't you wait for a while ?" begged
the boy, and his heart began to beat.

Then the little girl laughed the more, and
rose up on her knees. " No—the goat is mine,"
said she, and threw her arm round his neck,
untied her garter, and bound it round.

Ovind looked on. She rose and began to
pull at the goat, but he wouldn't go, and
stretched his neck over towards Ovind. " Ba-
a-a," said he. She took hold of him by the
hair with one hand, and drawing the cord in
with the other, said coaxingly,—" Come now,
goaty, come, you shall come to the kitchen and

I'll give you nice milk and bread,"—then she sang :

> " Come calf from my mother,
> Come goat from the lad,
> Come pussy mew kitty,
> Oh ! I am so glad !
> Come-ducklings so yellow,
> Go each with your fellow, .
> Come chickens and run,
> Haste to join in the fun,
> Come little doves cooing,
> Your feathers are fine—
> The grass may be wet,
> But the sun will still shine,
> Early, early, early, in the summer sky,
> Calling unto autumn that her days are nigh !"

There stood the boy. He had tended the goat since winter when he was born, and the idea of losing him had never entered his mind, but now he was gone all in a minute, and he should never see him more.

The mother came singing up from the well. She saw the boy sitting in the grass crying, and went over to him. "What are you crying for ?"

" Oh ! the goat,—the goat."

" Yes, where is the goat ?" said the mother, as she looked up to the roof.

" He won't come any more !" said the boy.

" Dear, how can that be ?"

Ovind wouldn't tell about it.

" Has the fox taken it ?"

" Oh ! I wish it was the fox !"

" Now what have you been doing ?" said the mother. " Where is the goat ?"

" Oh ! oh ! oh ! ......I...I...sold the goat for a biscuit !"

Just as he said the words, he felt what it was to sell the goat for a biscuit, he had not thought about it before. The mother said, " And what do you say now the little goat thinks of you, that you could sell him for a biscuit?"

· Now the boy fully understood it, and he felt sure he could never more be happy here,—not even with God, he thought again.

He felt so grieved, that he made an agreement with himself that he would never do wrong any more,—he wouldn't cut the spinning thread, and he wouldn't lose the sheep, nor go down to the sea alone. And as he lay, he fell asleep, and dreamt that the goat had gone to heaven ; the Lord sat there with a great beard as in the catechism, and the goat stood and nibbled the leaves from a shining tree, but Ovind sat alone upon the roof and couldn't come up.

Suddenly he felt something wet against his ear, and started up. " Ba-a-a !" it said. It was the goat come back again.

" Oh, are you come again !" He sprang up, took both the goat's forelegs, and danced with him as a brother ; he pulled him by the beard, and was just going in with him when he heard something behind, and turning, he saw the little girl sitting on the greensward. Now he understood it, and let the goat loose. " Is it you who have brought him back ?"

She sat and pulled the grass up. "They wouldn't let me keep him. My grandfather's up there waiting."

Just then they heard a shrill voice calling, —"Now!" Then she remembered what she had to do. She rose and went to Ovind, put one hand in his, looked down, and said : "Forgive me." But then her courage failed her; she cast herself over the goat, and wept.

"You shall keep the little goat," said Ovind, and turned away.

"Be quick!" said the grandfather up from the hill.

Marit rose and walked slowly on.

"You've forgotten your garter," cried Ovind.

She turned herself, looked first on the garter and then on him, and at last mumbled—"You can keep that."

He went and took her by the hand,—"Thank you!" he said.

" Oh, nothing to thank me for," she replied, heaved a deep sigh, and went away.

But Ovind wasn't so happy with the goat as he had been before.

CHAP. II.

AT SCHOOL.

BY the cottage side the goat was tethered, but Ovind was looking up towards the hill. His mother came and sat by him; he wished to hear stories about things far away, for the goat could no longer satisfy him. So he was told how once all things could speak,—the mountain spoke to the brook, and the brook to the river, and the river to the sea, and the sea to the sky; but then he asked if the sky spoke to nothing, —yes, the sky spoke to the clouds, and the clouds to the trees, and the trees to the grass, and the grass to the flies, and the flies to the

animals, and the animals to children, and
children to old people, and so it went again
and again, and round and round, and no one
knew who began. Ovind looked on the mountain, the trees, the sea, and the sky, and had in
reality never seen them before. The cat came
out and laid herself on the doorstep in the sun..
"What does pussy say?" said Ovind, and
pointed. The mother sang :

> " Softly the sun sheds his evening rays,
> Idly the cat on the doorstep lays.
>> ' Two little wee mice,
>> Some cream from a cup,
>> And a dainty fish slice
>> Have I eaten up,—
>> And I feel too lazy to stir,
>> I can only sit here and purr,'
>> Says the cat."

The cock with all his hens passed by. "What
does the cock say?" asked Ovind, and clapped
his hands. The mother sang :

> " Kindly the hen-mother spreads out her wings,
> Proudly the cock stands on one leg and sings,—

' Up in the air with plumage grey,
The wild goose swiftly his course may steer,
But, in intellect tell me I pray
Can he ever match with Sir Chanticleer !
Come, come my hens, to rest, to rest—
Soon will the sun sink down in the west,'
Says the cock."

Two little birds sat and sang up on the roof. " What do the little birds say ?" asked Ovind, and laughed.

"' Oh ! how pleasant and sweet is life
Free from the turmoil of constant strife,'
Say the little birds."

And so he got to hear what all things said, even down to the ant that crept through the moss, and the worm that bored in the bark.

The same summer his mother began to teach him to read. He had often wondered how it would be when the books began to talk, and now all the letters were animals, birds, or any-thing else he thought of ; but soon they began to go together two and two ; A stood and leaned against a tree, and called to B, then E

came and did the same, but now there were
three or four together, and it seemed as if they
disagreed,—the further he went the more he
forgot what they were. He could remember A
the longest, for he liked it the best, it was a
little black lamb and was friends with everybody; but soon he forgot A too. The book
had no stories, but was simply lessons.

One day his mother came in, and said to him
"To-morrow the school begins again, and I shall
take you there to the farm." Ovind had heard
that the school was a place where little boys
played together, and he had nothing to say
against it. He was delighted, and ran on before
his mother up the hill, full of glee and expecta-
tion. They reached the school-house, and a
busy hum greeted their cars, like the sound of
the water mill at home. He asked what it was.
" It is the children reading," she said : then he
was pleased, for he had read that way himself
before he knew his letters. When he came in

there were as many children sitting round the
table as he had ever seen at church. Others sat
on their dinner tins round the room, and some
stood in small groups before a black board.
The schoolmaster, an old grey-headed man, sat
on a stool by the fire filling his pipe. When
Ovind and his mother entered, they all looked
up, and the murmur ceased, as if the mill stream
were suddenly dammed. The mother said
" Good morning," and shook hands with the
schoolmaster.

" Here I come with a little boy who will
learn to read," said the mother.

" What's the bairn's name ?" said the schoolmaster, as he delved in his pouch for the tobacco.

" Ovind," said the mother ;" he knows his
letters and a few short words."

" Oh ! indeed !" said the schoolmaster.
" Come here you little white head !"

Ovind went to him, the schoolmaster lifted

him on to his knee, and took off his cap.
" Here's a nice little lad !" said he, and stroked
his hair.

Ovind looked up in his face and smiled.

" Is it me you're laughing at ?" and he
frowned.

" Yes, that it is," replied Ovind, and laughed
aloud. Then the schoolmaster laughed also,
and the mother, so the children saw they might
join, and they all laughed together.

This was the way in which Ovind entered
the school.

When he had to take his seat each one
wanted to make room for him, but he stood
looking round and round, from side to side,
with his cap in his hand and his book under
his arm, while they whispered and pointed.

" What then ?" said the schoolmaster, and
he took his pipe again.

As the boy turned round to the schoolmaster
he caught sight of Marit with the many names,

sitting on a little red painted box in the chimney corner : she hid her face in both her hands and sat and peeped at him.

" I'll sit here !" said Ovind quickly, hopped across the room, and set himself down by her side. Now she lifted her arm and looked at him from under her elbows ; then he did the same. This went on till they all laughed again.

" Be quiet, you naughty, troublesome, giggling gewgaws !—Come be good little children now !"

It was the voice of the schoolmaster, who, if he stormed, was sure to be calm before he finished.

The children were soon quiet again, until each began to con his lesson aloud. Then the treble voices sounded high, while the bass drummed louder and louder to overpower them, and one and another chimed in between, till Ovind thought he had never had such fun in all his days.

"Is it always like this?" he whispered to Marit.

"Yes, it's always like this," she said.

By and bye they had to go up to the school-master to read, then a little boy was set to hear them, and they soon found a chance to slip back to their corner again.

"I've got a little goat now, too," said Marit.

"Have you?"

"Yes, but it's not so nice as yours."

"Why haven't you come up oftener to the ridge?"

"Grandfather was afraid lest I should fall down."

"But it isn't so high."

"Grandfather won't let me come though."

"My mother knows so many songs," said Ovind.

"Oh! so does grandfather."

"Yes, but not the same as mother sings."

"Grandfather knows a dancing song!—Will you hear it?"

C

" Oh yes !"

" Then come further away so that the schoolmaster shan't see us."

He came quite close to her, and she said the
song over and over again, till he knew it by
heart, and this was the first that he learnt at
the school,—

> " Dance ! cried the fiddle
> In tuning the strings,
> Then suddenly upsprings
> A youth and cries ' Ho !'
>
> ' Hey !' said Erasmus,
> Embracing fair Randi,
> ' Come hasten to give me
> The kiss that you owe !'
>
> ' Nay,' answered Randi,
> But slipped away shyly,
> And nodding, said slyly,
> ' From that you may know !'"

" Up youngsters," cried the schoolmaster,
" this is the first day at school, and you may
go early, but now we must have prayers and
singing." Up rushed the children, laughing and

talking and scampering over the floor. " Silence! you little good-for-nothing chatter-boxes,—be good and walk nicely over the floor my children!" said the schoolmaster, whereupon they quietly took their places, the schoolmaster went in front and said a short prayer, and then they sang. He led in a deep bass voice, and all the children stood with folded hands. Ovind and Marit stood near the door—they also folded their hands, but they could not sing.

So ended the first day at school.

CHAP. III.

THE SCHOOLMASTER'S STORY.

VIND grew, and became a promising lad. At school he was always among the first, and at home he was industrious, for at home he loved his mother and at school the schoolmaster. He did not see much of his father, who was either away fishing or else attending to the mill.

That which at this time had the most influence over his mind, was the history of the schoolmaster, which his mother told him one night as they sat over the log fire. It entered his books, it peeped out of every word the schoolmaster said, and crept stealthily round

the school-room when all was still. It made
him obedient and respectful, and, as it were,
enlarged the powers of his mind. The story
ran thus:—The schoolmaster's name was Baard,
and he had one only brother called Anders.
They were much attached to each other, they
enlisted together, served in the same company,
were together in the war, and were both made
corporals ; and, when after the war they returned home, they were looked upon by everybody as two brave fellows.

Soon after this their father died, leaving a
good deal of property not easy to divide. To
overcome the difficulty, they resolved to have
an auction sale, when they could share the
profits, and each could buy those things he
liked best. Now the father had left a large
gold watch, known through all the country side,
for it was the only gold watch the people there
had ever seen. When this watch was put up
at the sale there were many bids, until both the

brothers began, and then others ceased.　Now Baard expected that Anders would let him have the watch, and Anders thought the same of Baard.　When the watch had come up to twenty dollars, Baard thought it wasn't nice of his younger brother, and he bid again until it was near thirty, but Anders would not give in. Then Baard said forty dollars at one bid, and looked no longer at his brother.　There was a deep silence in the room, broken only by the auctioneer quietly naming the last bid.　Anders thought that if Baard could afford to pay forty dollars, he could do it equally as well, and if Baard would not let him have the watch, he should pay dearly for it, so he bid higher. Then Baard laughed—" A hundred dollars and my brotherhood into the bargain," he said, and went out.　A moment after, as he saddled his horse, one came out and said to him, "The watch is yours ; Anders gave in."　As he heard this, a deep pang shot through him,—he thought of his brother and not of the watch. The horse was saddled, but he seemed uncertain whether to ride or not. Just then many of the people came out, and Anders among them, who, seeing Baard with his horse ready saddled and little dreaming of his real thoughts, called out aloud,—

" Thank you, Baard, you shall never see the day when I come in your way again !"

" Nor you the day when I set foot on this farm," retorted Baard, pale as death, as he swung himself into the saddle.

Neither of them ever trod again upon the threshold of their father's house.

Soon after this Anders got married, but Baard was not invited to the wedding.

During the same year, Anders' only cow was found dead close to his house, and no one could tell how it happened. One misfortune followed another, and everything seemed to go wrong ; at last, in the middle of the Winter, his hay loft and everything in it was burnt to the ground, and it could not be found out how the fire originated. " Some one who wishes me evil has done this," said Anders, and he wept. He was now reduced to poverty, and all his energy for work was gone.

The next evening Baard appeared at his brother's house ; Anders was lying down, but sprang up at the unexpected sight.

" What do you want here ?" said he, then stood fixedly gazing at him.

Baard waited a little before he answered, " I came to help you, Anders; you are in trouble."

" Things have gone with me as you would have them, Baard ! Go, or I cannot restrain myself."

" You are mistaken, Anders, I regret..."

" Go Baard, or we are both victims !"

Baard retreated a few steps, then in a trembling voice he said,—" If you would like the watch you shall have it."

"Go, Baard!" screeched the other, and Baard went.

Now with Baard things had been thus:—Finding his brother fared so ill, his heart was softened, but pride held him back. He felt a desire to go to church, and there he made good resolutions, but failed in carrying them out. He often went so near that he could see the house, but either some one came out at the door, or there was a stranger, or Anders stood and chopped wood,—there was always something in the way. But one Sunday in the Winter, he again went to church, and Anders was there too. Baard saw him, he looked very pale and thin, and he wore the same clothes he had done when they lived together, but now they were old and worn. During the sermon he looked up at the pastor, and Baard thought he seemed good and kind, and he remembered their child-hood's years and what a good lad he had been.

Baard himself went up to the altar that day,

and he made the solemn promise before God,
that he would be reconciled to his brother cost
him what it might.

This resolution took hold of him in the same
moment as he drank of the wine, and when he
rose he meant to go and sit by his brother, but
some one was in the way, and Anders did not
look up. After service there were also hinder-
ing things,—there were so many people,—his
wife walked beside him, and Baard did not know
her ; he thought it would be best to go home to
him alone, and talk openly with him.

When evening came, he went. As he reached
the room door, he listened, and heard his own
name mentioned ; it was by the wife.

" He came up to the altar to-day," said she,
" he was certainly thinking of you."

" No, he never thought of me," said Anders,
" I know him ; he thought only of himself."

Then there was a long pause ; Baard felt the
sweat upon his brow, although the night was

cold. He heard the wife busy with the kettle ; the fire blazed and crackled, a little baby cried now and then, and Anders rocked the cradle.

Then she said these few words,—" I believe you both think of each other without admitting it."

" Let us talk of something else," said Anders.

Soon after, he rose and went towards the door ; Baard hid himself in the stick house, but just there Anders came to get wood. Baard crouched in the corner, and could see him distinctly ; he had doffed the poor clothes he wore at church, and had taken instead the uniform he had brought home from the war, the same as Baard's, and which they had promised each other never to use, but to descend as heirlooms in the family. Anders' was now all patched and torn. His strong well-built body seemed enveloped in a bundle of rags, and at the same moment Baard heard the gold watch ticking in his own pocket. Anders went to the spot where the

wood lay, but instead of taking it he stood and
leaned against the pile, and gazing up into the
heavens, where the stars shone bright and clear,
he gave a sigh and said, "Yes,—yes,—yes,—
my God ! my God !"

So long as Baard lived these words sounded
in his ears. He stepped forward towards him,
but just then his brother coughed, and it felt so
hard that he stopped. Anders took the bundle
of wood, and passed so close to Baard that the
branches touched his face. There he stood,
without moving, till a cold shudder ran through
him. This aroused him ; he went out, and con-
fessed to himself that he was too weak to face
his brother, and he therefore resolved upon
another plan. In the corner of the stick-house
he found a few pieces of charcoal ; then he
selected a piece of fir wood for a torch, went up
to the hay-loft, and struck fire. When he had
got the torch lighted, he sought for the nail
where Anders would hang his lamp when he

came in the morning to thrash. On this nail Baard hung the gold watch, blew out the light, and went down ;—he felt so light-hearted that he sprang over the snow like a young lad.

The day after, he heard that the hay-loft had been burnt down the same night. Undoubtedly a spark must have fallen from his torch while he turned to hang up the watch.

This overpowered him so that he sat all day as though he were ill ; then he took the psalm book out and sang, so that the people in the house could not think what was the matter. But in the evening he went out. It was bright moonlight ; he made his way to the ruins of the hay-loft, and groped among the ashes. There, sure enough, he found a little lump of gold ;—it was the watch.

It was with this in his hand, he went to his brother that evening as before related, and sought for a reconciliation.

A little girl had seen him groping among the

ashes. He had also been observed going towards the farm the foregoing Sunday evening ;
the people in the house told how strangely he
had behaved on Monday ; everybody knew that
he and his brother were not on good terms, and
he was reported and brought up for trial.
Nothing could be proved against him, but sus-
picion rested on him, and now more than ever
it seemed impossible to approach his brother.

Though Anders had said nothing, he had
thought of Baard when the hay-loft was burnt,
and when the evening after, he saw him enter the
room looking so pale and strange, he at once
concluded that now remorse had struck him,
but for such an offence, and against his own
brother, there was no pardon. On hearing the
circumstantial evidence against him, though
nothing had been proved at the trial, he firmly
believed that Baard was guilty. They met each
other at the trial, Baard in his good clothes, and
Anders in threadbare. Baard looked up as he

went in, with so imploring a glance that Anders
felt it deeply. "He does not want me to say
anything," thought Anders, and when he was
asked if he believed his brother guilty, he
answered clearly and decidedly, "No."

From that day Anders took to drinking, and
matters grew worse and worse with him. With
Baard it was little better, although he never
drank ; he was not like himself.

Late one evening a poor woman entered the
little room where Baard lived, and begged him
to go with her. He knew her : it was his
brother's wife. He understood the errand she
had come upon, turned deadly pale, and followed without a word. There was a flickering
light from the window of Anders' room that
served to guide them, for there was no pathway
over the snow. They reached the house and
went in. On entering, Baard felt at once that
here reigned poverty ; the room was close ; a
little child sat on the hearth eating a piece of

charcoal : its face was black all over, but it looked up with its white teeth and grinned. There on the .bed, with all sorts of clothes to cover him, lay Anders, thin and worn, with his clear high forehead, looking mildly upon him. Baard trembled in all his limbs, he sat down on the bed foot, and burst into tears. The sick man continued silently looking at him. At last he told his wife to withdraw, but Baard signed to her to remain, and the two brothers began to speak together. They related each his history, from the day when they bid on the watch to the time they now met together, and it was clearly shown that during all these years they had never been happy for a single day. Baard finished by taking out the little lump of gold, which he always carried about with him.

Anders was not able to talk much, but as long as he was ill, Baard continued to watch by his bedside. " Now I am perfectly well," said Anders, one morning when he awoke,—" Now, my brother, we will always live together as in the olden time !" But that day he died.

Baard took the wife and the child to live with him, and they were well cared for from that time. That which the brothers had said to each other was soon known through the village, and Baard became the most esteemed man among them. Everybody met him as one who had known great sorrow and again found joy, or as one who had been long absent. Baard felt strengthened by all this friendliness around him, he loved God more, and felt a desire to be useful ; so the old corporal became a schoolmaster. That which he impressed first and last upon his pupils, was love, and this precept was so exemplified in himself, that the children were attached to him as to a play-fellow and father at the same time.

This was the story told of the old schoolmaster that had such effect upon Ovind, that it became to him both religion and education.

He looked upon the schoolmaster as a being almost supernatural, although he sat there so familiarly and corrected them. Not to know his lessons was impossible, and if, after saying them well, he got a smile or a stroke of the head, he was glad and happy for the whole day.

It always made a strong impression upon the children when, before singing, the schoolmaster would sometimes speak a little to them, and, at least once a week, read aloud a few verses about loving your neighbour. As he read the first of these verses his voice trembled, although he had now continually read it for twenty or thirty years. It ran thus :—

> " Be kind to thy neighbour and scorn him not,
> Though virtue and beauty be all forgot,
> And no light is seen from above ;—
> Remember he too has a soul to save,
> He must live again when beyond the grave,
> Then forget not the power of love !"

But when the whole of the piece was said, and he had stood still a little while, he looked at

them and blinked with his eyes,—" Up children,
and go nicely and quietly home,—go nicely, that
I may hear nothing but good of you, bairns !"
Then, while they hastened to find each his own
things, he called out through the noise,—" Come
again to-morrow, come in good time, little girls
and little boys, that we may be industrious."

CHAP. IV.

TWO BRIGHT BUTTONS AND ONE BLACK.

F his life, till one year before confirmation, there is not much to relate.
He read in the mornings, worked in
the afternoons, and played in the evenings.

As he was very lively the children of the
neighbourhood sought his company during play
hours. Close to the farm lay a great hill, as before mentioned, where, on a fine day, they
assembled to drive their sledges on the snow.
Ovind was always master in the field: he had
two sledges, "Quick Trotter," and "Superior."
The last he lent out, and the first he used himself, taking Marit with him.

The first thing Ovind did when he awoke in the morning, was to look out and see if it was fine weather; if it was thick and misty, or he heard it dripping from the roof, he dressed as slowly as if there was nothing to be done that day. But on the contrary, and especially on holidays, if it was sharp, cold, and clear weather, —his best clothes and no work, the whole of the afternoon and evening free,—hey! he bounded out of bed, was dressed like lightning, and could scarcely eat anything for excitement. When afternoon came he sprang over the hill to the sledge ground, and joined the party with a long shout that echoed from cliff to cliff, and the sound died far away. Then he looked for Marit, and when he found her there, he did not take much more notice of her.

Now one Christmas the boy and the girl were both about sixteen or seventeen years of age, and they were both to be confirmed in the Spring. In Christmas week there was to be a grand party at Heidegaard, where Marit's grand-parents lived, who had brought her up and educated her. They had promised her this fête for three years, and now at last they were obliged to fulfil their word. To this party Ovind was invited.

It was a dull evening, not a single star to be seen; it would probably rain next day. There were great drifts of snow along the mountain side, with here and there bare places, and again the groups of birch trees standing isolated and conspicuous against the white back ground. The farmstead lay in the middle of the fields on the mountain side, and in the darkness the houses looked like black clumps from which the light streamed first from one window then from another. It seemed as though they were busy inside. Old and young flocked thither from different directions. No one liked to go in first; so when they reached the farm, instead of going direct to the house, they loitered about the outbuildings. Some hid behind the cattle shed, a few under the granary, some stood beside the hay-loft and imitated foxes, while others replied in the distance as cats ; one stood behind the bakehouse and howled like an angry old dog, until there was a general chase. The girls came by-and-bye in great numbers, accompanied by their younger brothers, who would fain conduct themselves as grown-up men. The girls were very shy, and when the older youths already assembled came out to meet them, they ran away in all directions, and had to be brought in one by one. A few there were who would not be persuaded to enter, till Marit came herself and bade them. Now and then there also came a few who had certainly not been invited, and whose intention had been simply to look on from outside, but who, seeing the dancing, at last ventured in just for one single turn. Marit invited those she liked best into the private sitting room where her grand-

parents sat, and they fared exceedingly well.
Now Ovind was not of the number, and this he
thought very strange.

The grand fiddler of the neighbourhood could
not come until late, so they had to content
themselves with the old gardener, known by the
name of "Grey Knut." He could play four
dances,—two Spring dances, a halling,* and a
waltz. When they tired of these, they made
him vary the halling to suit a quadrille, and a
Spring dance in the same way to the mazurka
polka.

The party being at her grandfather's house,
Marit was dancing nearly all the time, and this
the more drew Ovind's attention to her. He
wished to dance with her himself, and therefore
he sat during one round in order to spring to her
side the moment the dance was done ; and this
he succeeded in doing, but a tall, dark-looking

---

* The "Spring dance" and "Halling" are the national
dances of the country.

fellow with black hair, stepped suddenly forward ;—" Away, child !" he cried, and pushed Ovind that he nearly fell over Marit. Never before had he known such behaviour,—never had any one been so unkind to him, and never had he been called " Child !" in that contemptuous way. He blushed crimson, but said nothing, and turned back to where the new fiddler, who had just entered, had seated himself, and now tuned up. Every one stood still, waiting to hear the first strong tones of " Himself ;" they waited long while he tuned the fiddle, but at last he began with a " Spring ;"—the lads stepped out, and, pair by pair, they quickly joined in the dance. Ovind looked at Marit as she danced with the dark-haired man ; he saw her smiling face over the man's shoulder, and for the first time in his life he felt a strange pang at his heart.

He looked more and more earnestly at her, and it came forcibly before him that Marit was now quite grown up. "And yet it cannot be," thought he, "for she is still playing with us in the sledges." But grown she certainly was, and the dark-haired man drew her to him at the end of the dance; she loosened herself from his clasp but continued to sit by his side.

Ovind looked at the man : he wore a fine blue cloth suit, and fancy shirt, and carried a silk pocket handkerchief; he had a small face, deep blue eyes, laughing defying mouth ; he was good looking. Ovind looked long at him, and at last he looked at himself. He had got new trousers for Christmas, which had much pleased him, but now he saw they were only of gray homespun ; his jacket was of the same material but old and dark ; his vest of common plaided cloth, also old, and with two bright buttons and one black. He looked round and thought very few were so poorly clad as he. Marit wore a black bodice of fine stuff, a brooch in her necktie, and had a folded silk pocket handkerchief in her hand. She had a little black head-dress fastened under the chin with broad striped silk ribbons; she was red and white; she smiled, and the man talked to her and laughed; the fiddler tuned up, and the dance must begin again.

One of his companions came and sat by him.

"Why don't you dance, Ovind?" he said kindly.

"Oh! no!" said Ovind, "I don't look like dancing."

"Don't look like dancing!" said his companion; but before he could get further, Ovind interrupted him,—

"Who is that in the blue cloth suit, dancing with Marit?"

"That is Jon Hatlen; he has been at the Agricultural School, and is now to take the farm."

At the same moment Jon and Marit seated themselves.

" Who is that light-haired lad sitting there by the fiddler and staring at me ?" said Jon.

Then Marit laughed and said, " Oh ! that's the peasant's son at the little farm."

Ovind had always known that he was a peasant's son, but until now he had never felt it. He felt now so insignificant, that in order to keep himself up, he tried to think of everything that had ever made him feel proud, from the sledge playing to the smallest word of commendation. But when he thought of his father and mother sitting at home, and picturing him happy and glad, he could scarcely refrain from tears. All about him were laughing and joking; the fiddler thrummed close under his ear; it seemed to darken before his eyes ; then he remembered the school with all his companions, and the schoolmaster who was so kind to him, and the pastor, who, at the last examination, had given him a book and said he was a clever lad ; his father even, who sat by, hearing it had given him a smile. " Be a good boy, Ovind," he could fancy he heard the schoolmaster say, taking him on his knee as though he were still a child. " Dear me, it is so small a matter, and in reality they are all kind, it only looks as though they were not,—we two shall get on Ovind, as well as Jon Hatlen, we shall get good clothes, and dance with Marit, a fine room, a hundred people, smile and talk together, go to church together, chiming bells, a bride and bridegroom, the pastor and I in the vestry, all with gladsome faces, and mother at home, a large farm, twenty cows, three horses, and Marit good and kind as at school......"

The dance over, Ovind saw Marit opposite to him, and Jon sat by her side, his face close to hers ; he felt again the sharp pain at his heart, and it was as if he said to himself,— " Yes, I am not well."

At the same moment Marit rose and came direct over to him. She bent down to speak to him,—"You must not sit and stare at me in that way," she said, "the people will notice it; now go and dance with some one."

He did not answer, but looked at her, and the tears came into his eyes. She had already turned to go, but observing it she stopped. She blushed crimson, turned and went to her place, then turned again and took another seat. Jon quickly followed her.

Ovind rose and went out; he passed through the house, and sat down on the steps of the adjacent porch, but did not know what he did it for. He got up, but sat down again, for he would not go home, and thought he might as well be there as anywhere else. He could not realise anything of what had happened, and he would not think about it, neither would he think of the future, it seemed so void.

"But what is it that I am thinking of?" he asked himself half aloud, and when he heard his own voice, he thought, "I can still speak; can

I laugh ?" And he tried : yes, he could laugh, and he laughed louder and louder, and then it seemed so curious to be sitting there quite alone and laughing, that at last he laughed at himself.

Now Hans his companion, who had been sitting by him in the dancing-room, had come out after him,—" Bless me, Ovind, what are you laughing at !" he exclaimed, and stopped in front of the porch.

Then Ovind ceased. Hans remained standing, as if waiting to see what would happen next. Ovind got up, looked carefully round, and then said in a low tone,—" Now I will tell you, Hans, why I have been so happy hitherto ; it is because I have not really cared for anybody ; from the day we care for any one we are no longer glad ;" and he burst into tears.

" Ovind !" a voice whispered out in the garden ; " Ovind !" He stood still and listened ; " Ovind !" it said again a little louder. It must be, he thought.

" Yes," he answered also in a whisper, dried his eyes quickly, and stepped forth. Then he saw a woman's figure slowly approaching,—

" Are you there ?" said she.

" Yes," he answered, and stopped.

" Who is with you ?"

" Hans."

Hans would go ; but Ovind said " No ! no !"

She now came slowly up to them ; it was Marit.

" You went so soon away," she said to Ovind.

He did not know what to reply. This made her feel embarrassed, and they were all three silent. Then Hans gradually withdrew. The two now stood alone, but they neither looked at each other nor moved. Then Marit said in a whisper, " I have gone the whole evening with this Christmas fare in my pocket for you, Ovind, but I have not been able to give it you before." She then drew out some apples, a slice of yule cake, and a little bottle of home-made wine, which she pushed to him and said he could keep.

Ovind took it. " Thank you," he said, and held out his hand ; her's was warm ; he let it go quickly as if he had burnt himself.

" You have danced a great deal this evening."

" I have so," she replied ; then added, " but you have not danced much !"

" No, I have not !"

" Why have you not ?"

" Oh !"

" Ovind !"

" Yes."

" Why did you sit and look at me so ?"

" Oh !"

" Marit !"

" Yes."

" Why did you not like me to look at you ?"

" There were so many people."

" You have danced a great deal with Jon Hatlen this evening !"

E

" Oh ! yes."

" He dances well."

" Do you think so ?"

" Don't you ?"

" Why yes !"

" I don't know how it is, but this evening I cannot bear to see you dance with him, Marit !"

He turned away; it had cost him much to say it.

" I don't understand you, Ovind."

" I don't understand it myself; it is stupid of me. Goodbye, Marit, now I must go."

He went a step without looking round ; then she called after him,—" It is a mistake that which you have seen, Ovind !"

He stopped,—" That you are grown up is at least no mistake," said he.

He did not say what she had expected, and therefore she was silent ; but at this moment she saw the light of a pipe before her ; it was her grandfather who had just turned the corner

and now passed by.   He stood still.   " Are you
there, Marit ?"

" Yes."

" Who are you talking with ?"

" Ovind."

" Who did you say ?"

" Ovind Pladsen."

" Oh ! the peasant lad at the little farm !—
Come in directly !"

CHAP. V.

A NEW AIM IN LIFE.

HEN Ovind awoke the next morning it was from a long refreshing sleep, and happy dreams. Marit had been on the mountain and tossed grass down upon him ; he had gathered it up and thrown it back again ; it went up and down in a thousand shapes and colours, the sun stood high in the heavens, and the whole mountain looked dazzling in its brightness. On awaking, he looked round to see it all again ; but then he remembered the events of the day before, and the same acute stinging pain at his heart returned. This will never leave me, he thought, and a feeling of helplessness came over him, as though the whole future were lost to him.

" You have slept long," said his mother, as she sat by his side and spun,—" Come now, and get your breakfast, your father is already in the forest, hewing wood."

It was as if the voice helped him ; he got up with a little more courage. It may be the mother remembered her own dancing time, for she sat and hummed at her wheel whilst he took breakfast. This he could not bear ; he rose from the table and went to the window ; the same heaviness and indifference possessed him, but he sought to overcome it by thinking of his work. The weather had changed, it was colder, and that which yesterday threatened for rain fell to-day in wet sleet. He put on his sailor's jacket and mittens, his gaiters, and a skin cap, then said "Good morning," and took his axe on his shoulder.

The snow fell slowly in great white flakes ;

he trudged laboriously over the sledge hill to enter the forest from the left. Never before, either Winter or Summer, had he passed over the sledge hills without some joyful remembrance or happy thought. Now it was a lifeless, weary way ; he dragged through the wet snow, his knees were stiff, either from dancing the day before or from lack of energy. He felt that the sledge play was at an end for this year, and, therefore, for ever. Something else he longed for, as he threaded his way among the trees where the snow fell noiselessly ; a frightened ptarmigan screamed and fluttered a few yards off, and everything seemed to stand as though waiting for a word that never was said. But what it was that he longed for he could not exactly tell, only it was not to be at home, nor was it to be anywhere else ; it was not pleasure, nor work, it was something high above or far away. Shortly after, it shaped itself into a definite wish ; it was to be confirmed in the

Spring, and there to be number one. His heart beat as he thought of it, and before he could hear the sound of his father's axe among the branches, this desire had stronger hold of him than any he had ever known since he was born.

As usual his father did not speak many words to him ; they both hewed, and threw the wood together in heaps. Now and then they came into close contact, and once Ovind let slip the unhappy words,—" A poor peasant has much to endure !"

" As much as others," said the father, spat on his hands, and took the axe again.

When the tree was felled, and the father dragged it to the heap, Ovind remarked,—" If you were a rich farmer you wouldn't have to slave so."

" Oh, well there'd be other things to trouble me then," he replied, and worked away.

The mother came up with their dinner, and they seated themselves. The mother seemed in good spirits, she sat and hummed, and beat her feet together to the time.

" What will you be when you grow up, Ovind ?" she said suddenly.

" Oh ! for a peasant lad there isn't much to choose," said he.

" The schoolmaster says you must go to the training school."

" Can one go there free ?" asked Ovind.

" The school fund pays," answered the father whilst he was eating.

" Would you like it ?" asked the mother.

" I should like to learn something, but not to be schoolmaster."

They were all three silent awhile, she hummed again, and looked round. Ovind went away and sat by himself.

" We don't need to take from the school fund," said she, when the lad was gone.

Her husband looked at her : " Poor people like us !"

" I don't like, Thore, that you should always give yourself out for poor when you are not so."

They both of them peeped to see whether the lad could hear them where he sat.

Then the father looked sharply at her. " Nonsense ! you don't understand things."

She laughed, then said seriously, " It seems like not thanking God that we have got on well."

" He can be thanked without wearing silver buttons," observed the father.

" Yes, but to let Ovind go as he went yesterday to the dance is not to thank Him."

" Ovind is a peasant lad."

" Yet he may dress decently when we can afford it."

" Say it so that he can hear it !"

" He can't hear, or else I should have a good mind to do it," she said, looking naively at her husband, as he glumly put his spoon away and took out his pipe.

" Such a poor farm we have," said he.

" I can't help laughing at you, you always talk of the farm and never speak of the mills !"

" Oh dear ! you and the mills ; I don't think you care whether they go or not."

" Yes, thank God, if they'd only go both night and day."

" But now they've been standing ever since before Christmas."

" No one grinds at Christmas time."

" They grind when there's water ; but since they got the mill up at Nystrommen, there's nothing to be done."

" The schoolmaster didn't say so to-day."

" H'm— I shall let a more discreet man than the schoolmaster manage our affairs."

" Yes, last of all he should talk with your own wife."

Thore did not reply to this, but lighting his pipe, he rose and leaned against the wood pile, looking first at his wife and then at his son, and finally fixing his gaze on an old crow's nest that hung deserted up in a pine tree.

Ovind sat by himself, with the future spread before him, like a long blank sheet of ice, along which, for the first time, he rushed restlessly from one side to the other. He saw clearly that poverty hemmed him in on every side, but this made him only the more determined to overcome it. From Marit it had certainly separated him for ever ; he half regarded her as engaged to Jon Hatlen ; but he resolved that with all his might he would strive to keep pace with them through life. Not to be any more humiliated as he had been yesterday, he would keep away, till, by God's help, he could become something more than he was at present, and he did not feel a doubt in his own mind but that he should succeed. He had a sort of feeling that he would do best to study, but what further that should lead to he must leave to the future.

There was capital sledge driving in the

evenings; the children all came to the hill, but not Ovind. Ovind sat by the fire and read, he had not a moment to spare. The children waited long for him; at last they became impatient, and one and another came and peeped in and called to him, but he pretended not to hear. Evening after evening they came and waited outside in wonderment, but he turned his back to them and read, paying no heed to their entreaties.

Later he heard that Marit had not been to the sledge playing either. He read with such diligence that even his father thought it went too far. He grew thoughtful; his face, which had been so round and mild, became thinner and sharper, his eyes deeper; he seldom sang and never played, it was as if time were too short. When the desire to join his old companions came over him, it was as if something whispered, "Not yet, not yet,"—and continually, "not yet." The children played, shouted, and laughed awhile as before, but when they saw they could not by any means induce him to come, they gradually disappeared ; they found other grounds and soon the sledge hill was quite vacated.

The schoolmaster soon observed that he was not the same Ovind who used to read because it fell out so, and play because it was necessary. He often talked with him, and sought to find the cause, for the lad's heart was not light as in former days. He spoke also with the parents, and by agreement he came one Sunday evening late in the Winter, and after sitting awhile, he said,—" Come, Ovind, let us go out, I want to talk with you a little."

Ovind got up and went with him. They took the path towards Heidegaard. The conversation did not flag, but they spoke of nothing important ; when they came near the farms, the schoolmaster took the direction of the middle one, and as they got nearer they heard the sound of laughter and merriment.

" What is up here ?" said Ovind.

" They are dancing," said the schoolmaster, " shall we not go in ?"

" No."

" Will you not go to a dance, lad !"

" No, not yet."

" Not yet ?   When then ?"

He did not answer.

" What do you mean,—not yet ?"

As he did not reply, the schoolmaster said,— " Come now, no such talk !"

" No, I won't go."

He was very positive and seemed agitated.

" That your own schoolmaster should stand here and have to ask you twice to go to dance !"

There was a long silence.

" Is there any one you are afraid of meeting ?"

" I cannot tell who there may be there."

" But could there be any one ?"

No answer.

Then the schoolmaster went close up to him, and laid his hand on his shoulder,—"Are you afraid of meeting Marit ?"

Ovind looked down, and breathed heavily and quickly.

" Tell me, Ovind."

Still no answer.

" You perhaps feel ashamed to confess it before you are confirmed, but tell me anyhow, and you will never regret it."

Ovind looked up but he could not say a word, and his eyes fell again.

" You are not light-hearted as you were ; does she care for any one more than you ?"

Ovind was still silent, the schoolmaster felt a little hurt, and turned away ; then they went back.

When they had gone some distance, the schoolmaster waited till Ovind got up to him,— " You wish very much that you were con-firmed," said he.

" Yes."

" What do you then intend to do ?"

" I should like to go to the Training School."

" And to be schoolmaster ?"

" No."

" You think it isn't good enough ?"

Ovind was silent.

" Then what would you be ?"

" I haven't thought much about it."

" If you had money I suppose you'd buy a farm ?"

" Yes, but keep the mills."

" Then it would be better to go to the Agricultural School."

" Do they learn as much there as at the Training School ?"

" No ; but they learn that which will afterwards be of use."

" Do they get numbers there ?"

" Why do you ask that ?"

" I should like to be amongst the first."

" You can be that without numbers."

They were silent again till they came in sight of the little farm ; they could see a light shining from the room ; the overhanging mountains looked black in the Winter evening, the lake below was one blank sheet of ice, and the moon reflected the shadow of the pine trees.

" It is a beautiful place !" said the schoolmaster.

Ovind could sometimes see it with the same eyes as when his mother told him stories, and as when they played with the sledges ; this he did now,—all looked pleasing and bright.

" Yes, it is beautiful," said he, but sighed.

" Your father has found it sufficient ; perhaps you might do so too."

The happy aspect of the place vanished at once. The schoolmaster stood as if waiting a reply, but getting none he shook his head and went in. He sat awhile with them, but was more silent than talkative. When he said good

F

night, the parents both rose and followed him out, as if expecting that he had something to say. They stood waiting, and looked out upon the night.

" It has grown so quiet," said the mother at last, "since the children left off playing here."

" You have no longer a child in the house," said the schoolmaster.

The mother understood him,—" Ovind has not been happy of late," said she.

" No, he who is ambitious is not happy," and he looked up calmly into the quiet heavens.

CHAP. VI.

NOT QUITE FAIR.

HALF a year after, in the Autumn, the confirmation being deferred till then, the candidates were all assembled in the school-room for examination, and among them Ovind Pladsen and Marit Heidegaard. Marit had just come down from the pastor, who had given her a book and much praise, and she laughed and talked with her friends on all sides. Marit was now quite grown up, free and easy in her manners, and the boys as well as the girls knew that Jon Hatlen, the first young man in the district was paying attention to her. She might well be glad they thought as she sat there.

Close by the door there stood a group of girls and boys who had failed in their examination, and these were crying, while Marit and her friends were laughing. Among them was a little boy in his father's boots and with his mother's church handkerchief,—"Dear, oh dear!" he sobbed, " I daren't go home again."

And those who had not yet been called up, were so affected by the power of fellow feeling that it caused a general silence. Fear seized them in the throat and eyes ; they could not see clearly, neither could they swallow, though feeling a constant desire to do so.

One sat and reckoned up how much he knew, and although a few hours before he had found he knew everything required, he now saw with equal certainty that he knew nothing ; he could not even read. Another called to mind all his wrong-doings from the earliest time he could remember, till now when he sat there, and he though it wouldn't be strange of God if He didn't let him pass. A third sat and took signs from everything around him. If the clock, which was on the point of striking, should not sound till he counted twenty, he would pass ; if the footstep he heard in the passage was that of the farm-boy Lars, he would pass ; if the great raindrop that ran down the window pane should get to the bottom, he would pass. The last and final proof should be, if he could get the one foot twisted right round the other, but this he always found to be impossible. A fourth felt sure that if they would ask him only about Joseph in the Bible history, and about baptism in the Catechism, or about Saul, or the Commandments, or about Jesus, or——he sat and was still proving himself, when he was called. A fifth had a strong partiality for the Sermon on the Mount, he had dreamt about the Sermon on the Mount, he was certain to be heard in the Sermon on the Mount ; he said it over to himself, and he thought to go out and read it over

again, when just then he was called up to be
questioned on the Prophets. The sixth thought
about the pastor, who was such a good man and
knew his father so well, and of the schoolmaster,
who had so friendly a face, and of God, who was
so really good, and had helped so many before
both Jacob and Joseph, and then he thought
that his mother and sisters at home would be
praying for him, and that would certainly help.
The seventh sat and gave up in despair all the
things he had thought he would be when he
grew up. Once he had thought of being a
general or a pastor, and once he had even
dreamt of being king, but now that time was
gone by. Up to the present he had thought of
going to sea, and of becoming captain, perhaps
a pirate, and thereby to attain great riches ; now
gave up first the riches, then the pirate, then
the captain, and the mate, and he stopped at
the common sailor, or, at the most, the boat-
swain, if ever he got to sea at all, but probably

he must just take a place on his father's farm.

The eighth was more confident of himself, but yet not sure ; the cleverest even was not sure He thought of the clothes he was to be confirmed in, and what they could be used for if he did not pass ; but if he passed he should go to town and get cloth clothes, and come home again at Christmas time and dance, to the envy of the youths and the astonishment of the girls. The ninth reckoned differently ;—he made up a small account book between himself and God. On the one side he wrote, "Debit ; He shall let me pass," and on the other side, "Credit ; so shall I never lie any more, nor tell tales ; always go to church, leave the girls to themselves, and never swear any more." The tenth thought that if Ole Hansen had passed last year, it would be more than injustice if he, who had always got on better at school, and besides was of better family, should not pass this year. By

his side sat the eleventh, who revolved in his
mind the most fearful plans of revenge in case
he should fail, either to burn the school down,
or else to leave the village and come again as
the thundering judge of the pastor and the
whole of the school commissioners, but proudly
to let mercy go before justice. To begin with,
he would take a place with the pastor in the
neighbouring district, and there be number one
next year, giving answers so as to astonish the
whole church.

The twelfth sat by himself under the clock,
with both his hands in his pockets, looking over
the assembly with a dejected and sorrowful air.
No one here knew what was his responsibility.
One at home knew it; he was betrothed. A
great daddy long-legs came crawling along the
floor near to his feet; he used to tread upon
the odious insect, but to-day he kindly lifted his
foot to let it go in peace whithersoever it
would. His voice was mild as a Collect; his

eyes said continually that all men were good ;
his hands slowly moved out of his pocket and
up to his hair, to smooth it down. If only he
could squeeze himself through this dangerous
needle eye, he would recover himself again at
the other side, smoke tobacco, and make his
engagement public.

Down on a low stool, with his legs crouched
up together under him, sat the uneasy thirteenth;
his small sparkling eyes looked round the whole
room three times in a second, and through his
strong rough head rushed all the thoughts of
the twelve in broken disorder, from the bright-
est hope to the most despairing doubt, from
the humblest promises to the most mighty plans
of revenge ; and, meanwhile, having bitten his
poor thumb so that he could bite no longer, he
began with his nails, and sent great pieces to all
parts of the floor.

Ovind sat by the window, having been up and
given correct answers to everything he had been

asked ; but neither the pastor nor the school-master had commended him, , though for a whole half-year he had been thinking what they both would say when they got to know how hard he had worked, and he felt very much dis-appointed as well as hurt. There sat Marit, who, for far less labour and knowledge, had re-ceived both encouragement and reward. It was just to be great in her eyes he had studied, and now she had reached laughing, the point he had toiled so hard to attain. Her laughter and joking touched him to the quick,—the easiness with which she moved wounded him. He had carefully avoided speaking to her since that evening ; years should pass first he thought, but the sight of her now, so bright and lively, pressed him down, and all his proud resolutions hung as wet leaves.

He sought little by little to shake it off; much, however, depended on his being Number One to-day, and to know this he waited anxiously.

The schoolmaster used to remain a little while with the pastor to consider the order in which the children should stand, and then he would come down and tell them the result; it was certainly not the final decision, but it was what they agreed upon together.

The conversation in the room became more and more lively as one after another was examined and passed; but now the ambitious began to separate themselves from those who were merely light-hearted. The latter either went at once to tell their parents and friends of their success, or they waited for their companions who had not yet been called up; the former, on the contrary, became more and more silent, their eyes directed constantly towards the door.

At last the young people were all ready, the last had come down, and the schoolmaster was consulting with the pastor. Ovind looked at Marit; she was one of those who had remained, but whether for her own sake or for others he knew not. How beautiful Marit had grown; exquisitely fine was her complexion; he had never seen its equal; her nose was well formed, her mouth smiling. Her eyes were dreamy when she was not directly looking at any one, but therefore her glance came with unexpected power when it did come; and she half smiled in the same, as if to say that she meant nothing by it. Her hair was more dark than light, it was wavy, and she wore long curls, which, together with the dreamy eyes, gave a depth and charm that captivated. One could not be certain who it was that she looked for, as she sat there among them all, nor what she really thought when she turned to any one to speak, for that which she gave she took as quickly back again. Under all this, Jon Hatlen is certainly hidden, thought Ovind, but yet he continued to look at her.

Then the schoolmaster came. They all with one accord rushed up to him.

"What number am I?" "And I?" "And I, I?"

"Silence! uproarious children,—no noise here; be quiet, and then I will tell you."

He looked slowly round him. "You are Number 2," he said to a lad with blue eyes looking beseechingly at him, and the lad danced out of the circle. "You are Number 3,"—he touched a red-haired quick little boy who stood and pulled at his coat; "You are Number 5;" "You Number 8," &c. He caught sight of Marit,—"You are Number One of the girls." She blushed crimson over her face and neck, but tried to smile. "You, Number 12, have been lazy, you idle worthless scamp;" "Number 11, you couldn't expect to stand higher, my lad;" "You, Number 13, must read diligently before the confirmation or else you won't succeed!"

Ovind could not bear it any longer. Number One had certainly not been named, and yet he had stood the whole time so that the schoolmaster

could see him. "Schoolmaster?" He did not
hear. "Schoolmaster!" Three times he had
to call before he was heard.

At last the schoolmaster looked at him—
"Number 9 or 10, can't say exactly which,"
said he, and turned quickly to another.

"Who is Number One then?" asked Hans, who
was Ovind's best friend.

"Not you, you curly head!" and tapped him
on the hand with a paper roll.

"Who is it then?" asked many. "Who is
it?" "Yes, who is it?"

"He will get to know it himself!" said the
schoolmaster decidedly. He would not have
more questions.

"Now go nicely home children, thank God,
and make your parents happy! Thank your
old schoolmaster too, if it had not been
for him you would not have been good for
much!"

They thanked him and laughed, then went

joyously home. One only was left, who could
not quickly find his books, and when he found
them, sat down as if to read again.

The schoolmaster went up to him, "Well
Ovind, are you not going with the others?"

He did not answer.

" Why are you opening your books again?"

" I want to see what it is that I've answered
wrong."

" You have not answered anything wrong."

Ovind looked at him, and the tears gathered
in his eyes, he turned his head away while one
after another rolled slowly down, but he did not
speak a word.

The schoolmaster went in front of him,—
" Are you not pleased that you have passed?"

His lips quivered, but he did not answer.

" Your father and mother will be very
pleased," said the schoolmaster, and looked at
him.

Ovind struggled some time to get a word.

out ; at last he asked in slow broken sentences, —" Is it—because I—am a peasant lad—that I am Number 9 or 10 ?"

" Surely it must be so," said the schoolmaster.

" Then it is no use for me to work," said he hopelessly, and all his grand dreams vanished. Suddenly he lifted his head, raised his right hand, struck it on the table with all his might, cast himself down on his face, and burst into a violent fit of tears.

The schoolmaster left him to lay there and cry it out; he waited long, till at last his grief became more childlike. Then he rose, took Ovind's head in both his hands, lifted it up, and looked into the tearful face.

" Do you think God has been with you ?" said he, as he looked kindly at him.

Ovind sobbed still, but not so violently, the tears ran more quietly, but he dare not look at him who spoke, nor reply.

"This, Ovind, has been a deserved reward ;

you have not read from love to religion, nor your parents, but you have read from vanity."

There was silence in the room between each time of the schoolmaster's speaking, and Ovind felt his glance to be resting upon him, and grew softened and humbled under it.

" With such angry feelings in your heart, you could not have stood forth to have made a compact with your God, could you Ovind ?"

" No," he stammered, as well as he could.

" And if you stood there conceitedly flattering yourself that you were Number One, would it not be wrong ?"

" Yes," he whispered, and his mouth quivered.

" You are still attached to me, Ovind ?"

" Yes." He looked up for the first time.

" Then I must tell you it was I who had your number placed low down ; because I care for you so much, Ovind."

The old schoolmaster looked at him, blinked a few times, and the tears ran quickly down.

G

" You have not anything against me for it ?"

" No." He looked up brightly though his voice trembled.

" My dear child, I will watch over you as long as I live."

He waited for him till he had gathered his books together, and then said he would go home with him. They went slowly along : at first Ovind was silent, battling with himself, but by degrees he overcame. He was convinced that that which had come to pass was the best that could have happened, and, before he reached home, this belief was so strong, that he thanked God, and told the schoolmaster so.

" Yes, now we shall hope to attain to something in life," said the schoolmaster, " better than running after blind men and numbers. What do you say to the Training School ?"

" Yes, I should like to go there."

" You mean the Agricultural School ?"

" Yes."

" That is certainly the best ; it gives other prospects than those of a schoolmaster."

" But how can I get there ? I do so wish it, but I have no means."

" Be industrious and good, and the means will be found."

Ovind was quite overwhelmed with gratitude. He felt the kindling in the eye, the light-heartedness, the endless fire of love, that comes when we experience the unexpected kindness of our fellow-men. The whole future presents itself for a moment, with that sort of feeling one has when walking in fresh mountain air, of being borne along rather than of walking.

When they came home, both the parents were in the sitting-room, quietly waiting there, though it was the busy time of the day. The schoolmaster entered first ; Ovind after; both were smiling.

" Now ?" said the father, laying aside a prayer-book, where he had just been reading a catechumen's prayer.

The mother was standing by the fire-place ; she smiled, but did not say anything ; her hands trembled, and she evidently expected good news though she did not wish to betray herself.

" I thought I must just come to give you the good news, that he has answered every question correctly, and that the pastor said, after Ovind was gone, that he had not examined a more promising candidate.

" Oh no !" said the mother, and was much moved.

"Well done !" said the father, and turned restlessly round.

After a long silence, the mother asked in a low voice, "What number is he ?"

"Number 9 or 10," said the schoolmaster quietly.

The mother looked at the father, who looked first at her and then at Ovind,—" A peasant lad cannot expect more," said he.

Ovind looked at him in return ; it was as if something would stick in his throat, but he forced it back by quickly thinking of one cheering thing after another.

" Now I must leave," said the schoolmaster, nodded, and turned to go.

As usual both parents followed him out ; then the schoolmaster taking a quid, said smiling, " He will be Number One after all, but it is better not to tell him till the day comes."

" No, no," said the father, and nodded. " No, no," said the mother, and nodded too ; then taking the schoolmaster's hand,—" Thank you for all you have done," said she. " Yes, thank you," said the father, and the schoolmaster went, but they stood long and looked after him.

CHAP. VII.

A VOICE FROM THE RIDGE.

THE schoolmaster had judged well when he asked the pastor to prove whether Ovind could bear to stand Number One. In the three weeks intervening between this time and the confirmation he was with the lad every day. It is one thing for a pure young heart to yield to an impression, and another to hold fast the good qualities he possesses. Many dark hours came to the lad before he learnt to build his future on better things than vanity and pride. When sitting at his work he would suddenly leave it, saying hopelessly,—"What is the use? What do I gain?" But then a minute after, he would remember the kind words and goodness of the schoolmaster, and so each time he lost sight of his higher duties, he was enabled, by these human means, to bring them into view again.

At the little farm they were preparing at the same time, for his examination, and for his journey to the Agricultural School,—as the day after the confirmation he was to set off. The tailor and the shoemaker sat at work in the loft, the mother was baking in the kitchen, and the father was busy with a trunk. They were querying as to how much it would cost them in two years, and whether he could come home the first Christmas, perhaps he could not even come the second, and how hard it would be to be so long separated. They spoke also of the love he should bear to his parents, when they strove so hard to put their child forward. Ovind sat as one, who in his first trial at sea, had upset the boat, and been picked up by kindly sailors.

Such a feeling brings humility, and with it many other things. As the great day drew near, he felt himself to be fully prepared for it, and looked hopefully to the future. Every time the image of Marit presented itself to his mind, he strove carefully to put it aside, though it always gave him pain to do it. By practice in it he sought to strengthen himself, but instead he felt only a deeper pain. Therefore he felt weary the last evening, when, after a long self-proving, he prayed to God that in this matter He would not try him.

The schoolmaster came in in the evening. They all sat together, after having prepared themselves as it is customary to do, the evening before taking the Sacrament. The mother was much moved, and the father was unusually silent ; separation lay behind the festival of the morning, and it was uncertain when they could all meet again. The schoolmaster took the Psalm-book, they had a little service and sang, and then he prayed from the heart as words came to him.

These four sat there until late in the evening ; they gradually grew silent, each occupied with his own thoughts ; then they separated with best wishes for the coming day, and the influence it would have.

Ovind thought when he went to rest that night that he had never been so happy before, and he gave his own special interpretation to it ; never before, thought he, have I laid down so desirous of fulfilling God's will and so trustful in it. Marit's face soon presented itself again, and the last he remembered was, that he lay and proved himself :—not quite happy, not quite ;— and that he replied :—yes, quite ;—but again :— not quite ;—yes, quite ;—no ; not quite.

When he awoke, he at once remembered what day it was ; he prayed, and felt refreshed, as one does in a morning. He rose in good time and carefully tried on his new clothes, for he had

never had such fine ones before. There was a
round jacket especially that seemed strange to
him ; it was made of fine cloth, and he felt it
again and again before he got used to it. When
he had put his collar on, and for the fourth time
tried on the jacket, he got hold of a little look-
ing-glass, and, catching sight of the beautiful
hair encircling his own self-satisfied face, it
suddenly struck him that this again was vanity.
Yes; but people may surely be well-dressed
and clean, he argued, as he turned away from
the glass as though it were sin to look in it.
Well, but not to think so much of themselves
for it. No, certainly, but the Lord must like
that one should care to be tidy. That may be,
but would He not like better that you should
look well without thinking so much about it.
Yes, but it's only because everything is so new.
Well then, by-and-bye you will forget it. Then
he began in the same way to prove himself
first upon one point and then upon another,

he felt so afraid lest any sin should blot that day.

When he came down his parents were all ready and waiting breakfast for him. He went up to them and thanked them for his new clothes; they wished him the customary, "Health to wear them and strength to tear them ;" then they seated themselves at the table, said grace, and began the meal. When they had finished, the mother cleared the table and brought in the lunch basket for the journey to church. The father put on his jacket, and the mother her shawl, they took the Psalm-books, locked up the house and set off. On reaching the main road they met with a great many going to church, some driving and some on foot, a few of the candidates for confirmation among them, and now and then white-haired grand-parents, who tried to get to church just this once again.

It was an Autumn day without sunshine as if the weather were about to break. The clouds met and parted again; great masses broke into small patches, chasing each other far away and bearing with them orders for rain; down on the earth it was still quiet, the leaves hung dead and motionless, the air was a little oppressive; the people carried cloaks but did not require to use them. A large concourse of people had gathered round the solitary church; but the confirmation candidates all went straight in, to be placed before the service began. Then the school-master in his blue dress coat and knickerbockers, high boots, stiff neck-cloth, and pipe sticking out of his pocket, walked about, nodding and smiling, patting one on the shoulder, and telling another to answer clearly and distinctly, until he reached the lower end where Ovind stood talking to his friend Hans, and answering all his questions about the journey. " Good morning, Ovind, you look very well to-day." He took hold of him by the coat saying confidentially, " I think a great deal of you; I have been talking to the pastor, and you are to have your right place as Number One ; go up and take it and answer well."

Ovind looked up astonished at him ; the schoolmaster nodded ; the lad went a few steps forward, then stopped, then a few more steps, then stopped again ; yes, it's true—he has spoken to the pastor for me,—and the lad went straight on.

" You are Number One after all," whispered one.

" Yes," said Ovind in a low tone, but scarcely knew yet whether he dare say it.

The placing being accomplished, and the pastor having come, the bell rung and the people streamed into the church. Ovind looked up and saw Marit Heidegaard standing straight opposite him. She also saw him, but they both of them felt so awed by the sacredness of the place that they dared not greet each other. He saw only that she was bright and beautiful, and that

she wore nothing on her head. Ovind, who for
half-a-year had had so many pleasant dreams
of standing opposite to her, now that it was
really come to pass, forgot both the place and
her.

When all was over, his relations and friends
came to offer their congratulations ; then his
companions having heard that he was to travel
next day came to say good-bye ; and many of
the younger ones, whom he had driven in the
sledges, and whom he had assisted at school,
cried a little at the thought of his departure..
At last Ovind and his parents left for home
accompanied by the schoolmaster. On the way
there were several more came to offer him their
good wishes and to take leave ; otherwise they
did not speak much till they sat again in the
quiet room at home.

The schoolmaster tried to help them to keep
their courage up, but now that it was come to
the point, they all three, never before having been

parted for a single day, dreaded the separation for two whole years, but none of them wished to shew their feelings. As the time passed on Ovind grew worse and worse, and at last he went out of doors to quiet himself.

It was growing dark, he stood upon the steps and looked up listening to the gentle sighing of the wind. Then he heard his own name called down from the ridge, quite softly, yet there was no mistaking it, it was repeated twice. He looked up, and could just discern a woman's figure looking down from among the trees.

" Who is that ?" he asked.

" I hear you are going away," she said in a low tone, " so I thought I would come and say good-bye to you, seeing you hadn't come to me."

" Dear, is that you, Marit ! I'll come up to you."

" No, don't, I've been here so long, and then I should have to stay still longer, and no one knows where I am, so I must be quick home."

" It was kind of you to come," said he.

" I couldn't bear that you should leave in that way Ovind ; we have known each other since we were children."

" Yes, we have."

" And now we haven't spoken to each other for half-a-year."

" No we haven't."

" We were separated so strangely that time too."

" Yes, I think I must come up to you."

" Oh no, don't ! but tell me, I hope you are not grieved with me ?"

" Dear, how could you think so ?"

" Good-bye then Ovind, and thank you for all the pleasant times we have had together !"

" Marit !"

" Yes, but now I must go, they will miss me."

" Marit,—Marit !"

" No, I daren't stay longer, Ovind ; fare-well !"

" Farewell !"

The rest of the evening he was, as it were, in a dream, answering absently when they spoke to him.   They attributed this to the thought of his coming departure, which was quite a natural thing, and which certainly did occupy his atten-tion at the moment when the schoolmaster took his leave, and slipped something into his hand, which he afterwards found to be a five dollar piece.   Soon, however, it passed out of his mind, and he thought only of the words that had come down from the ridge and gone up again.

II

CHAP. VIII.

BE SURE THAT YOU BURN IT.

DEAR PARENTS,—We have a great deal more to read now, but as I am much more up to the others, it is not such hard work. When I come home I shall make great changes in father's farm, for there is a great deal that is very bad, and it is a wonder that things have hung together as they have. But I shall put all to rights, for I have learnt many things here. I should like to be in a place where I can have things as I now know they should be; so when I am ready I must seek for a good situation. All here say that Jon Hatlen is not so clever as they think at home, but he has his own farm, so that is no matter. Many who come from here get a very high salary, and they are so well paid because this is the best agricultural school in the country. Some say that there is a. better in the next county, but that is not true.

There are two words here, the one is called Theory, and the other Practice ; one is nothing without the other, but it is well to know them both ; the last, however, is the best. Theory is to know the reason why a thing should be done, and practice is to be able to do it. Here we learn both. The Principal is so clever that no-body can come up to him. At the last General Agricultural Meeting he brought forward two subjects for discussion, while the principals from the other schools had none of them more than one, and in the discussions they found he was always right. But the last meeting, when he wasn't there, ended in nothing but talk. The lieutenant, who teaches us surveying, was engaged only because he is so very clever ; the other schools have no lieutenant.

The schoolmaster asks if I go to church ; yes, certainly I go to church, for now the pastor has got a curate who preaches so that everybody is terrified, and it is a pleasure to hear him. He comes from the college in Christiania, and people think he is too strict, but it is good for them.

At present we are reading history that we have never read before, and it is wonderful to see all that has happened in the world, especially in our country, for we have constantly conquered except when we have lost, and that has been only when we haven't been equal. Now we have more liberty than any other country except America, but there they are not happy ; and our liberty we must prize above all things.

Now I must conclude for this time, for I have written a great deal. The schoolmaster will read this letter, and when he answers for you, ask him to tell me some news about one or another, for this he doesn't do.

With best love,

Your attached son,

OVIND THORESEN PLADSEN.

DEAR PARENTS,

I must now tell you that we have had an examination, and I stand very high in many things. I am high in writing, and land measuring, but not so good in composition. The principal says this is because I have not read enough, and he has given me some books by Ole Vig, which are very easy to understand.

Everything here is so small to what it is in other countries ; we understand next to nothing, we learn everything from the Scotch and Swiss, but gardening most from Holland.

I have now been here nearly a year, and I thought I had learnt a great deal ; but when I saw what those who left at the last examination knew, and thought that not even they knew anything in comparison to the foreigners, I felt quite disheartened. I am now in the first class, and must stay here another year before I am ready. But most of my companions are gone, and I long for home. It seems as if I stood alone, though I certainly do not, but it feels so strange when one has been long away.

What am I to do when I leave here ? I shall naturally come home first, and then I must seek for some situation, but it must not be far away.

Good-bye dear parents. Remember me kindly to those who ask after me, and say I am well, but I long to come home.

Your attached son,
OVIND THORESEN PLADSEN.

DEAR SCHOOLMASTER,

This is to ask you if you will be so good as to send the enclosed letter, but be sure and say nothing about it to anybody. If you will not, then it must be burnt.

OVIND THORESEN PLADSEN.

To MARIT KNUDSDATTER HEIDEGAARD.

You will very likely be surprised to receive a letter from me, but you need not be, for I will only ask how you fare, and this you must let me know as soon as possible and in every respect.

Respecting myself, I have only to say that I shall be ready to leave here in one year.

Respectfully,

OVIND PLADSEN.

To OVIND PLADSEN,

At the Agricultural School.

I duly received your letter from the school-master, and will answer it as you ask me, though I am rather afraid, because you are now so learned ; I have a letter book but it doesn't suit. However, I will do my best, and you must take the will for the deed ; but you musn't show it, or else you are not what I think you are ; and you musn't hide it because any one might easily get hold of it, but you must burn it, that you must promise me.   There are a great many

things that I wanted to write about, but I dare
not. We have had a good Autumn; potatoes
are high, and here at Heidegaard we have plenty
of them. But the bears have made sad havoc
among the stock this Summer; they killed two
of Ole Nedregaard's cows, and injured one of our
tenant's calves so that it was obliged to be killed.

I am weaving a very large web like the Scotch
plaid, and it is very difficult. And now I must
tell you that I am still at home, though there
are some who would have it otherwise.

I have nothing more to say this time, and so
good-bye.

MARIT KNUDSDATTER.

You must be sure to burn this letter.

To OVIND THORESEN PLADSEN.

I have said to you Ovind, that he who walks
with God shall have a good inheritance. And
now listen to my advice : look not to the world
with too much longing and anxiety, but trust
in God and let not your heart be discouraged.

Your father and mother are both well, but I suffer a good deal, for now I feel the effects of the hardships I endured in the war. That which you sow in your young days you reap in your old, both in body and soul, and this is now my experience. But the aged should not complain, for sorrow teacheth wisdom, and affliction worketh patience, and strengthens for the last journey.

There are many reasons why I take the pen to write to you to-day, but first and foremost on Marit's account, for she has grown a good girl, though she is light of foot as a reindeer and is changeable. She would wish to keep to one, but it is not in her nature. I have often observed that with such tender hearts the Lord is merciful and lenient, and does not suffer them to be tempted above that they are able to bear.

I duly gave her the letter and she hid it from all but her own heart. If the Lord will further this matter I have nothing against it. That she finds approbation in the eyes of the young men can easily be seen, and she has abundance of this world's goods and also of the heavenly, but with the latter there is much unsettledness ; the fear of God with her is like water in a shallow dam, it is there when it rains but away when the sun shines.

Now my eyes will not bear any more, for though I can see pretty well at a distance, they begin to water when I look closely at anything. Finally, let me remind you, Ovind, whatsoever you aspire to, take counsel of God, as it is written :—" Better is an handful with quietness, than both the hands full, with travail and vexation of spirit."—(Proverbs IV. 6.)

Your old schoolmaster,

BAARD ANDERSEN OPDAL.

TO MARIT KNUDSDATTER HEIDEGAARD.

Thanks for your letter, which I have read, and burnt as you told me to do. You write a great deal, but you don't say anything about that I

want you to, and I dare not write about a certain matter until I know how you fare in every
respect.

The schoolmaster says nothing to be depended
upon, he praises you, but he calls you wavering.
That you were before. Now I don't know what
to believe ; you must write, for I shall feel uneasy until I have heard from you. Just now I
often think of that last evening when you came
to the ridge, and of what you then said.

I will not write more this time, so good-bye.

With all respect,

OVIND PLADSEN.

To OVIND THORESEN PLADSEN.

The schoolmaster has given me a fresh letter
from you, which I have now read, but I cannot
understand it, which must be because I am not
learned. You want to know how I fare in every
respect. I am quite well. I have a good appe-
tite and sleep at nights, and sometimes also in
the day. I have danced a great deal this

Winter, for there have been many delightful
parties here.   I go to church when there is
not too much snow, but it has been very thick.
Now you must have heard everything, but, if
not, I don't know anything better than that you
should write to me again.

MARIT KNUDSDATTER.

TO MARIT KNUDSDATTER HEIDEGAARD.

I have received your letter, but you appear to
wish me to remain as wise as before.   Perhaps
this is an answer after all, I don't know.   I dare
not venture to write that which I wish to, because I don't feel to know you.   Perhaps you
don't know me any better.   You must not think
I am any longer the soft fellow that you crushed
the spirit out of, as I sat and watched you dance;
I have had many provings since then.   Neither
am I, as I used to be, like those long-haired
dogs that hang their ears and shun people ;. but
enough of this now.

Your letter was humorous enough, but the joking

was just where it should not have been, for you understood me quite well, and you should have known that I did not ask in joke, but because lately I have not been able to think of anything else than that I asked you about. I waited anxiously, and then there came nothing but foolery.

Farewell, Marit Heidegaard. I shall take care not to look too much at you as I did at that dance. Grant you may both eat well and sleep well, and get your new web finished, and grant above all, that you may shovel away the snow lying before the church door.

With all respect,

OVIND THORESEN PLADSEN.

To OVIND THORESEN.

In spite of my age and the weakness of my eyes, together with the pain in my hip, I must yet give in to the entreaties of the young, for they are glad to make use of the old people when they stick fast themselves. They call and cry till they are let loose, and then they run away again and will not hear us any more. This time it is Marit, who, with many coaxing words, has begged me to write a letter to send with hers, as she dare not trust herself to write alone. She had thought she had Jon Hatlen or another fool to deal with, and not one that schoolmaster Baard had brought up, but now the matter has come to a critical point. Yet you have been a little too hard, for there are some women who joke to keep from weeping. I am glad, however, that you look at serious things seriously, otherwise you could not laugh at that which is laughable. The position in which you stand to each other, is now apparent from many things. I have often had my doubts about Marit, for she is variable as the wind, but now I know she has refused Jon Hatlen, and greatly enraged her grandfather thereby. She was pleased when she received your letter, and it was not to repulse you that she wrote jokingly.

She has suffered much, and that in waiting for the one she cared for, and now you will not have her but set her aside as a foolish child.

This was what I had to say to you, and if you take my advice you ought to be at one with her, for you will find enough besides to trouble you. I am like an old man who has seen three generations ;—I know folly and its reward.

Your father and mother send their best love to you : they long to see you back. I have always avoided speaking of this before, lest it should make you home-sick. You do not know your father, and when you really learn to know him, you will marvel. He has been depressed and silent in respect of his affairs, but your mother made his mind easy, and now things look brighter.

Now my eyes grow dim, and my hand is un-steady, so I commend you to Him whose eye is ever watchful and whose hand stayeth not.

BAARD ANDERSEN OPDAL.

To Ovind Pladsen.

I am grieved that you are vexed with me, for I didn't mean it as you have taken it. I am aware I have not always acted rightly towards you, and I wish to tell you so, but you must not show this to any one. · Once when I got what I liked I wasn't good, and now no one cares for me any more, and I'm very unhappy. Jon Hatlen has written a song about me, and all the lads sing it, so that I daren't go anywhere. Both the old people know about it, and they are very cross. I am writing this alone, and you mustn't show it to any one.

I have often been down to see your parents. I have spoken with your mother, and we understand each other now, but I cannot tell you more for you wrote so strangely last time. The schoolmaster only makes game of me, but he knows nothing about the song, for no one dare sing such before him. I stand alone and feel to have no one to talk to. I often think of the time when we were children, when I always rode on your sledge, and you were so good to me. I could wish we were children again.

I dare not ask you to answer me any more, but if you will write just this once I shall never forget it, Ovind.

                    MARIT KNUDSDATTER.

P.S.—I beg you burn this letter, I scarcely know if I dare send it.

DEAR MARIT,

It was a happy moment when you wrote that letter ; and I thank you for it.

I feel as if I could scarcely stay here any longer Marit, I love you so much, and if you love me as truly, then Jon Hatlen's song and others' bitter words shall be like the chaff that the wind blows away. Since I received your letter I am like another man,—I feel so much stronger, and am not afraid of anything in the whole world. After I had sent my last letter I regretted it so, that it made me almost ill,

I

and now you shall hear what this led to. The
principal took me aside and asked me what was
the matter; he thought I read too much. Then
he said to me that when my year here was completed, he would allow me to stay a year longer
free of expense; I should assist him in several
ways, and he would give me a chance of learning
more. Then I thought that work was the only
thing for me, and I was very grateful, and even
now, though I long so much to come to you,
I do not regret it, for it will put me in a better
position for the future. How happy I am! I
do the work of three, and shall never be behind
in anything. I will send you a book I am reading, for there is a great deal about love, and I
read it at nights when the others are asleep; then
I read your letter over too.

Have you thought of the time when we shall
meet again? I think about it very often, and
so must you, it is so delightful. I am glad I
wrote so much before, though it was so difficult,

for now I can open my whole heart to you.   I
shall send you several books to read, that you
may see what those who truly love each other
have had to go through, choosing rather to die
of sorrow than to give each other up.   And we
should do so too.   Though it will be two years
before we see each other, and longer still before
we really belong to each other, we must cheer
our hearts by thinking that each day as it goes
brings us one day nearer.

I have a great deal to write about, but I will
leave it till next time, as I have not got any
more paper to night, and the others are all asleep.

Now I shall go to bed and think of you till I
sleep.

Your friend,

OVIND PLADSEN.

CHAP. IX.

OVIND THROWS HIS CAP IN THE AIR.

NE Saturday, at Midsummer, Thore 'Pladsen rowed over the lake to meet his son, who was coming that afternoon from the Agricultural School. The mother had had a charwoman for two or three days, and everything was made beautifully clean and tidy. Ovind's room had been ready some time, and the stove was set in order. To-day his mother decorated it with green, took the linen up, and made the bed, looking out between times over the water, to see if there was not a boat. The table was ready spread, and yet there was always something to be done,—flies to chase away, or dust, constant dust.

Still there was no boat. She seated herself in the window sill and looked out; then she heard footsteps on the other side and turned to see who was there; it was the schoolmaster, who came slowly along leaning upon a stick for his hip was very bad. He stopped a minute to rest, the expressive eyes moved quietly round ; he nodded to her : " Not come yet ? "

" No, I am expecting them every moment."

" Good hay weather to-day."

" But very hot for old people to be out."

The schoolmaster smiled : " Has somebody else been out in the heat to-day ? "

" Yes, but she's gone again."

" Oh ! well, may be they'll be meeting somewhere to-night."

" I suppose so, but Thore says they shall not meet in his house till the old people give their consent."

" Quite right."

"They are coming, I do believe !" the mother exclaimed."

" Yes, that is them."

The schoolmaster came in and rested a little, and then they went down to the lake, while the boat plied quickly along, for both father and son were rowing. When they came near, Ovind turned, rested his oars, and called "Good morning, mother ; good morning, schoolmaster !"

"What a manly voice," said the mother, "but still the same light hair," she added.

Ovind sprang out, and shook hands ; he laughed, and so unlike the peasants' way, he at once began to tell them all about the examination, the journey, the principal's testimonial, his prospects, &c. ; then he asked about the harvest, and about his friends, all except one. And so they went home, Ovind laughing and talking ; the mother smiling, not knowing exactly what to say ; the schoolmaster and the father listening. Ovind was pleased with everything he saw,—first, that the house was painted; then, that the mill was enlarged ; then, that the lead windows were taken out of the parlour, and white glass put instead of green.

When they came in, everything looked so exceedingly small, so different from what he had remembered it ; but so cheerful, and all looked so inviting.

They seated themselves at the table, but there was not much eaten, for Ovind was constantly talking. Once when he was telling them a long story about one of his schoolfellows, and there came a moment's pause, his father said, "I can scarcely understand a single word of what you say, lad, you speak so exceedingly quick." They all laughed, and Ovind not the least ; he knew it was true, but he seemed as though he could not help it.

All that he had seen and heard during his long absence, had so impressed and aroused him, that the powers which had hitherto lain dormant were now awakened, and the brain was constantly at work.

He was delighted with his little room ; he thought he should like to stay at home for a time, assisting with the hay harvest and reading; where he should go after he could not tell, but it was all the same to him. They were afraid lest he should have grown thoughtless, but on the contrary he remembered everything ; and it was he who thought of the boat and unpacked the things. He had gained a quickness and power of thought that was quite refreshing, and a liveliness in expressing his feelings, which, during the whole year, had only been repressed.

The schoolmaster looked ten years younger. "Now we have come so far with him," said he, as he rose to go.

The mother called Ovind aside, "Some one expects you at nine o'clock," she whispered.

"Where ? "

"Up on the ridge."

Ovind looked at the clock, it was nearly nine.
He could not wait in the house, but went out,
clambered up the ridge, and looked round. The
house roof lay close below; the bushes on the
roof were very much larger, and all the small
trees had grown; he could remember each one.
And there lay the road, grey and sombre, and
the wood with its varied foliage, and in the bay a
vessel laden with planks, waiting for wind. The
lake was bright and calm; some sea-birds flew
over, but did not cry as it was late. He sat
down waiting; the small trees prevented him
from seeing very far over, but he listened to the
slightest noise. For some time there were only
birds that started up and deceived him; then
again, a squirrel springing from tree to tree.
But at last he heard a rustling, then it ceased;
then it came again. He rose,—his heart beat
fast, the blood rushed into his head; there was
a movement in the bushes close to him, and a

shaggy dog appeared ; it was the dog from
Heidegaard, and close behind, it rustled again ;
the dog looked back and wagged his tail ; now
comes Marit.

A bush caught her dress, she turned to release
it, and so she stood when he first saw her ; she
had her hair plainly dressed, as was the custom
with the peasant girls on week days; she wore
a strong plaided dress without sleeves, and
nothing on her neck except the linen collar.
She had stolen away from her work, and durst
not stay to tidy herself. She looked up and
smiled, then she came forward, growing more
and more red at each step. He went to meet
her, and took her hand in both of his; she looked
down, and so they stood.

"Thanks for all your letters," was the first he
said, and when she then looked up a little and
laughed, he felt that she was the most roguish
little elf he ever could meet in a wood ; but he
was caught, and she not any the less.

"How you have grown!" she said, but meant something quite different.

They looked at each other but said nothing. Meanwhile the dog had seated himself at the edge of the ridge, and looked down upon the farm, and Thore observing his head from below, could not for his life think what it could be.

When, at last, the two began to talk, Ovind spoke so quickly that Marit couldn't help laughing.

" Yes, you see, it's when I am glad, really glad, you see, and when we came to understand each other it was as if a lock sprang open within me, sprang open, you see."

She laughed, then she said, " I know all the letters you sent me by heart."

" And I know yours too, but you always wrote such short letters."

" Because you always wanted them so long."

" And when I wanted you to write about one

particular thing, you slipped away, and I never heard how you got rid of Jon Hatlen."

" I laughed."

" How ? "

" Laughed, don't you know what it is to laugh?"

" Yes, I can laugh ! "

" Let me see ! "

" Did you ever hear such a thing ! I must have something to laugh at first."

" I don't need it when I am happy."

" Are you happy now, Marit ? "

" Do I laugh now, then ? "

" Yes, that you do !"

He took both her hands, and clapped them together as he looked at her. Here the dog began to growl, then his hair stood on end, and he barked, and grew more and more angry till at last he seemed quite savage. Marit sprang up in fear, but Ovind went forward and looked down. It was his father the dog was barking at; he was standing close under the ridge, with both his hands in his pockets.

" What ! are you there, too ? Pray, whose is that savage dog ?"

" It's a dog from Heidegaard," replied Ovind, rather taken aback.

" How in the world did it come there ?"

The mother hearing the noise, had come out to see what it was, and understanding at once how things were, she laughed, and said : " The dog comes here every day, so it's nothing wonderful."

" But what a ferocious animal !"

" He'll be quiet if he's spoken to," said Ovind, and patted him. The dog ceased barking though he continued to growl. The father was satisfied and went down again.

" Safe this time !" said Marit, " but there's some one else to watch us."

" Your grandfather ?"

" Exactly."

" But that won't do any harm."

" Not the slightest."

" You promise me ?"

" Yes, I do Ovind."

" How pretty you are, Marit ! "

" So said the fox to the raven, and got the cheese."

" You may think I want the cheese too."

" But you won't get it."

" I shall take it then."

She turned her head, and he didn't take it.

" I'll tell you something, Ovind," and she looked slily round.

" Well."

." How ugly you have grown."

" You'll give me the cheese though."

" No, indeed I won't," and she turned away again.

" Now, I must go, Ovind."

" I'll go with you."

" But not out of the wood, or grandfather will see you."

" No, not out of the wood,—dear, are you running ? "

" We cannot go side by side here."

" But this isn't to go in company."

" Catch me then," and on she ran.

They stopped when they got to the end of
the trees.

" When shall we meet again ? " she whispered.

" To-morrow, to-morrow."

" Yes, to-morrow."

" Good bye ;" she ran.

" Marit ! " and she stopped.

" How strange that we should meet first up
on the ridge."

" Yes, it is ; " she ran again.

He looked long after her,—the dog ran before
and barked, she after, trying to silence him. Ovind
took his cap, and tossed it again and again ;
" Now, I believe, I really begin to be happy,"
said he, and sang as he went home.

CHAP. X.

TURN THE RIVER WHERE IT CAN FLOW.

HEN they were all making hay, one afternoon, in the summer, a little bare-headed, bare-footed boy came running down the ridge over the field to Ovind, and gave him a note.

"You are running fast," said Ovind.

"Yes, I am paid for it," answered the boy.

Ovind was a little perplexed when he opened the note, it was so carefully wrapped up and sealed; it ran as follows :—

"He is on his way now, but he goes slowly. Go into the wood and hide.

YOU KNOW WHO FROM."

" No, that I won't," thought Ovind, and looked defiantly up over the hill.

It was not long before an old man came into sight on the top of the hill; resting, then going a little further, and resting again. The father and the mother both left off working to look at him. Thore smiled; but the mother, on the contrary, changed colour.

" Do you know him ? "

" Yes, there's no mistaking him."

The old man came slowly nearer and nearer. He was somewhat tall and burly, and being rather lame, he could only with difficulty walk by the help of his staff. When he came close to, he stopped, took off his cap, and wiped his forehead. His head was quite bald at the back; he had a round tight-drawn face, small piercing eyes, bushy eyebrows, and a full row of teeth. He spoke in a sharp shrill voice, hopping, as it were, over gravel and stone, and every now and then resting with great delight upon an inviting

J

R.   In his younger days he had been known
as a cheerful, but hot tempered, man; now, after
many adversities, he had grown peevish and
distrustful.

Thore and his son had many journeys backwards and forwards before old Ole got up to
them, but at last, as they came out from the hay
loft, they saw him standing in front of the
kitchen door, as though doubtful what to do; he
held his cap and staff in one hand, and with the
other wiped his bald head with a handkerchief.
Ovind stood behind his father as he went up
and accosted him.

"You must be tired, will you not come in?"

Ole turned and looked sharply at him, at the
same time adjusting his cap, before he replied:

"No, I can rest where I stand, I shall not be
long."

Since he had lost his hair his cap was far too
big for him, it came down over his eyes; so that
to be able to see, he had to hold his head right back.

"Is that your son standing there behind you?" he began in a harsh voice.

"They say so."

"His name is Ovind, is it not?"

"Yes, they call him Ovind."

"He has been to one of those Agricultural Schools in the south, hasn't he?"

"Yes, something of that kind."

"H'm, my girl, my granddaughter, Marit seems to have lost her senses in these latter days."

"That's a pity."

"She will not marry."

"What?"

"She wont have any of the fine young men who come to pay their addresses to her."

"Indeed?"

"And it is his fault, his that stands there."

"Indeed?"

He has completely turned her head, that son of yours, Ovind."

" Do you say so ? "

" See now, I dont like that any one should take my horses when I let them go to the mountains; and neither do I like that any one should take my daughters when I let them go to the dance, don't like it at all."

" No, of course not."

" I cannot go after them, I am old, I cannot take care of them."

" No no, no no."

" You see I wish to keep order, and when I say a thing must be done, it must, and when I say to her, not him, but him, it must be him, and not him ! "

" Certainly ! "

" But it is not so; for three years she has said no, and for three years there hasn't been a good understanding between us. That is not good, and if it is he who is the cause of it, I will only say to him, so that you hear it, you who are his father, that it is no use, he must give up."

"Well."

Ole looked a minute at Thore, then said, "You give such short answers."

" I can't make the sausage longer than it is."

Here Ovind must laugh, though in sooth he was in no laughing mood; but with some people laughter and fear go hand in hand.

" What are you laughing at?" said Ole sharply.

"I ?"

" Are you laughing at me ?"

" Heavens preserve me!" but his own reply only made him worse.

Ole saw this, and it infuriated him. They would turn the conversation, and begged him to go in, but it was three years' pent up anger that now sought liberty, and it was not to be stayed.

" Don't think to make a fool of me," he began, " I seek my granddaughter's happiness as I understand it, and your giggling laughter shall not hinder me. One doesn't bring up a girl just to

hand her over to the first peasant that turns up,
neither does one labor for forty years to leave
all to the first that fools her. My daughter went
on so, till at last she married a scamp; he ruined
them both through drink, and I had to take the
child, and pay for the entertainment, but, on my
word, it shall not be so with my granddaughter, do
you hear that ? I tell you that as true as I am
Ole Nordistuen of Heidegaard, the priest might
as well think of publishing the banns for the
trolls up in the forest, as to give out such names
from the pulpit as Marit's and your's, you puppy
dog! You sly fox, as if I didn't know what
you think of, you and she ! You think old Ole
must soon turn his nose up in the church-yard,
and then you'll trip away to the altar. No, no,
I've lived seventy years now, and you shall see,
boy, that I shall not die till you are both tired
out ! I tell you, you may watch for her, and not
even see her footprints, for I shall send her away
somewhere where she will be safe, and you may

roam about like a fool, and keep company with the wind and the rain! And now I shan't say any more to you, but you, who are his father, know my will, and if you desire his happiness in this respect, you will get him to turn the river where it can flow, for through my territory it shall not pass." He turned, and hobbled away with short quick steps, lifting the right foot higher than the left, and grumbling to himself.

An evil foreboding overshadowed those who remained; there was no more joking and laughter and the house stood as though empty. They entered without a word being said. The mother, who had overheard all from the kitchen door, looked at Ovind sorrowfully, almost in tears, and would not make matters harder for him by saying anything. The father sat down in the window, and looked after Ole. Ovind watched for the slightest change of expression on that grave and serious face, for on his first word the destiny of the future might depend. If Thore should join Ole in saying no, it would hardly be possible to overcome it. His frightened thoughts bore him swiftly on from one obstruction to another. He saw before him only poverty, opposition, and misunderstanding, and each support that he had relied on seemed to give way under the thought. It increased his anxiety that his mother stood with her hand on the door-latch, uncertain whether to stay and see the result or not, and that at last she quite lost courage and stole quietly out. Thore was still staring out of the window, and Ovind dared not speak to him, for he knew he must have his thought out. Just then, his own thoughts having run their unhappy course, took courage again, and, as he looked at his father's knitted brows, he thought : "None but God can separate us in the end." Thore drew a long sigh, he rose, and at the same time met his son's gaze. He stopped, and looked long at him: "I should like it best if you could give her up, for one should not either beg, or force oneself upon others ; but if you cannot, you must let me know, and perhaps I can help you." He went to his work, and the son followed.

In the evening Ovind had got his plan all ready. He would try to get to be Agriculturist for the district, and would ask the principal and the schoolmaster to help him. "If she will hold out, by God's help I shall win her through my work."

He waited in vain for Marit that evening, but whilst he waited he sang the song he loved the best :—

> " Come lift your head up, my thoughtful lad,
>   If a hope from your heart be riven,
> Another may brighten your tearful eye,
>   If you turn to the light of heaven !
>
> Come lift your head up, and look around,
>   Voices are kindly calling,—
> A thousand voices are bidding you come,
>   Softly their echoes are falling !
>
> Come lift your head up, for deep within
>   Lieth a fountain of blessing,
> Tones of music are flowing free,
>   Love on your heart impressing.

Come lift your head up, and gaily sing,
　Nor fear for the coming morrow,—
As the buds of the Spring return again,
　So joy will come after sorrow.

Then lift your head up, and courage take
　In the hope around you springing,
From the blue above, to the green beneath,
　To the world she ever is singing.

CHAPTER XI.

GATHERING BERRIES.

IT was in the middle of the noonday's rest ; the people at Heidegaard were asleep, the hay lay scattered about the field, and the rakes were all stuck in the ground. The hay sledges stood outside the granary, and the horses were grazing a little distance off. Except these, and some hens that had strayed in the corn field, there was not a living thing to be seen.

The road from the farm to the rich grass fields of the Heidegaard Sœters,* lay through a moun-

---

* To those of our readers who have travelled in the mountain-ous districts of Norway, the idea of the " Sœters " is sure to

tain pass. Up in the pass a man stood and looked down over the plain, as though expecting something. Behind him lay a tarn, from which the beck flowed down, that had made the cleft in the mountain. On both sides of the lake there were sheep walks leading to the Sœters, which he could see far in the distance. The barking of dogs and the tinkling of bells resounded among the rocks ; the cows were rushing madly to the water, while the poor

---

convey a romantic and pleasing impression, and though to others we fear we cannot give a just representation of these strongholds of the brownies, we may at least explain the meaning of the word.

In the prospect of the long winter before them, the farmers are anxious to cultivate as meadow every available spot of grass land in the valley, and therefore during the summer months the cattle are sent to graze up in the forests and on the mountain sides, where each farm has its Sœter usually several miles away from the farm itself. A part of the family take up their residence in the small wooden house prepared in the simplest way for their accommodation ; a few plain wooden chairs and a table may be all the furniture, but everything is scrupulously clean, and here many a young girl may gain her first experience in housekeeping and the superintendence of the dairy.

herdsmen and the dogs sought in vain to gather
them. The cows appeared in the most wonderful shapes, with their tails in the air, kicking and
plunging, roaring and bellowing; making straight
for the lake, where, to their delight, they stood
quite still, up to their necks in water; their bells
tinkling with each move of the head. The dogs
drank a little, but kept back on the dry land;
the herdsmen came after, and seated themselves
on the warm smooth mountain side. Here they
took out their provision, exchanged with each

Early in the morning, when the dewy freshness of the air
gives life and vigour to all around, the milkmaid will arise, and
in clear beautiful tones sing a song of the country, and gather
the cattle around her, giving to each a handful of salt, and
calling them all by name. The mountains rise on all sides, and
her song is re-echoed from cliff to cliff. Far in the distance
amid the towering peaks, peep here and there the deep crevasses
filled with everlasting snow; the icy surface gives a glacier-like
appearance, and there you may see grand images of the sun
reflected like gigantic stars.

The herdsmen up in the Sœters play skilfully upon a curious
wooden instrument, peculiar to the country. This can be heard
for miles, and should any of the cattle have strayed from the
rest, they are guided back by the sweet sounds of the " Luur."

other; praised each others' dogs, oxen, and people; finally undressed and sprang in the water. The dogs wouldn't go in, but drawled lazily about, hanging their heads, with their tongues out on one side. There was no bird to be seen, no sound to be heard save the voices of the lads and the tinkling of the bells; the ling was burnt up and withered; the sun scorched the whole mountain side, and the heat was intense.

Ovind sat a long time in the hot sun, close to the beck that flowed from the lake; he waited and waited, but still there was no one to be seen at Heidegaard, and he began to be a little anxious, when suddenly a great dog came panting out from a door, followed by a young girl in summer attire; she sprang over the fields up towards the mountain. Ovind felt a strong desire to halloo but dare not; he kept a look out to see if any one should accidentally come out from the farm and see her, but she escaped unobserved. At last she got near, picking her way by the side of the brook, and helping herself on by the small bushes, the dog a little before her, snuffing in the air. Ovind ran to meet her, the dog growled and was hushed down, and as soon as Marit saw him come, she seated herself on the Great Stone, looking fiery red, and quite overpowered by the heat. He sat down beside her.

" I'm so glad you've come."

" How fearfully hot ! Have you been waiting long ?"

" No.—As they watch us so in the evenings, we must take the mid-day ; but after this, I think we ought not to keep things so secret, and it is just about this I wanted to speak to you."

" Not secret ? "

" I know very well that it suits you best to keep everything secret, but to shew courage suits you also. I have come to-day to talk a long time with you, and now you must hear."

" Is it true that you mean to try to be District Agriculturist ?"

" Yes, and I hope to succeed too. I have a two-fold object in view,—first, to gain position ; and secondly, to do something that your grandfather can both see and understand. It happens most fortunately that most of the farmers about Heidegaard are young people who wish to make improvements and require assistance; they have also means at command. So I shall begin there. I shall improve everything from the smallest things to the greatest. I shall give lectures, and also work ; and so to say, lay siege to the old man by good deeds."

" Well done, Ovind ! What more ?"

" The next concerns ourselves,—you must not go away."

" When he commands it ? "

" And keep nothing secret respecting us two."

" When he tortures me ?"

" But we gain more, and protect ourselves

better by having everything open. We shall be just so much observed by people, that they will talk of how much we care for each other, and they will the sooner wish us well. You must not leave. There is danger for those who are separated lest slander should come in between them ; they believe nothing the first year, but they begin little by little to be influenced the second. We two must meet when we can, and laugh away all the ill report they will set between us. We shall be able to meet at a dance now and then, and swing merrily round while they sit by who calumniate us. We shall meet at church, and talk to each other in the face of those who wish us a hundred miles away. If any one writes a ditty about us, we will see if we cannot write one in reply. No one can harm us if we keep together and let people see it. All the unhappiness in love belongs either to those who are afraid, or to those who are weak, or to those who are ill, or to those calculating people

K

who watch for certain opportunities, or to those
cunning people who at last suffer for their own
devices, or to those matter-of-fact people who
don't care so much for each other, that state and
position can disappear; they steal quietly away,
and send letters, and tremble at a single word,
and at last take that constant restlessness and
uneasiness for love ; they feel unhappy and
dissolve away like sugar. Pooh, pooh! if they
really cared for each other they would have no
fear, they would be light hearted, they would
not care who saw them. I have read about it in
books. I have seen it myself also ; that is a
poor love that goes round about. True love
must begin in secrecy because it begins in reserve
and modesty, but it must live in openness because
its existence is joy. It is as in the spring time,
when the leaves begin to shoot, all that is withered
and dry falls off from the tree as soon as the
new life begins. He who falls in love leaves the
useless toys he has held to before, the new life

springs, and then can no one see it? Hey, Marit! they will be glad through seeing us glad. Two betrothed, who are true to each other, are a benefit to the public, for they read them a poem which the children learn by heart, to the shame of their calculating parents. I have read of many instances, and there are rumours of such even here in the district, and it is just the children of those who once caused all the misery, that now speak of it and are moved by it. Well, now let us join hands, and promise to be true to each other and we shall succeed."

He was about to embrace her but she turned her head away, and slipped down from the stone. As he remained sitting, she came back again, and with her arms resting on his knees she stood there, and talked to him as she looked up.

"Listen now, Ovind, when he says I must leave, what shall I say?"

"You must say no, straight out."

"Oh dear! will that do?"

"He cannot take and carry you out to the carriage."

"If he doesn't do just that, there are many other ways in which he can force me."

"I do not think so. Obedience is certainly your duty so long as it is not sin ; but it is also your duty to let him know fully how hard it is to you to obey in this case. I think when he hears that, he will reconsider the matter ; for at present, like most others, he believes it to be only child's play. You must show him it is something more."

"You may think he is not easy to do with ; he watches me like a tethered goat."

"But you break the chain again and again in one day."

"That is not true."

"Yes, every time you secretly think of me, you break it."

"Yes, that way, but are you certain that I think of you so often ?"

" Were it else, you would not be here now."

" Oh ! but you sent me a message to come."

" But you came because your thoughts drove you."

" Rather because it was a fine day."

" You said just now it was too hot."

" To go up the hill, yes ; but down again ? "

" Then why did you come up ? "

" To be able to run down."

" Then why are you not going ? "

" Because I wish to rest."

" And talk to me about love ? "

" I couldn't deny you that pleasure."

" While the little birds sang,"—

" And all were asleep ; "

" And the bells they rang,"—

" O'er the green wood's steep."

Here they both saw Marit's grandfather come limping out on the farm, and go to the bell string to ring the people up. The people came slowly down from the out-houses, drawled sleepily

to the horses and rakes, scattered themselves
in various parts of the field, and soon all was
life and work again. The grandfather only
went out of the one house and into the other,
and at last up on to the top of the hay loft and
looked all round. A little lad came bounding
up to him, apparently he had called him. The boy
went down in the direction of Pladsen, and the
grandfather, in the meantime, went round about
the farm, often looking up to the mountain, but
little suspecting that the dark spot on the " great
stone" was Marit and Ovind. But again Marit's
dog brought misfortune, for seeing a strange
horse drive into Heidegaard, he seemed to
think it part of his business to bark at the
top of his voice. They tried to quiet him,
but he had got roused, and would not give
over ; the grandfather stood below and stared
straight up. But matters grew still worse, for
the sheep dogs hearing the voice of a stranger,
ran up, and seeing a great wolf-like champion,

these straight-haired Finnish dogs all united against him, and so frightened Marit, that she ran away without even saying good-bye; while Ovind, in the midst of the battle, kicked and struck, but only succeeded in driving the dogs further away, for they soon found themselves another battle field; he after them again, and so on, till at last they were close to the edge of the beck; here Ovind rushed on them again, and got them all into the water, just where it was really deep; and they crawled out, looking quite ashamed, and going each his own way; so ended the fray.

Ovind went straight over till he reached the high road, but Marit met her grandfather a little above the farm, and the dog was to blame for this.

"Where have you been?"

"Into the wood."

"What have you been doing there?"

"Gathering berries."

"That is not true."

"No, it isn't."

"What did you do then?"

"I was talking to some one."

"Was it the peasant lad?"

"Yes."

"Listen now, Marit, you are going away to-morrow."

"No."

"Well, Marit, I will only say one single thing, you SHALL go."

"You can't lift me into the carriage."

"No? Can't I?"

"No, because you won't do it."

"Won't I? Listen, Marit, only for pleasure you see, only for pleasure, I will give that rag-gamuffin a real good thrashing."

"No, you daren't do that."

"Don't dare? Do you say I dare not? Who could do anything to me, who?"

"The schoolmaster."

" The schoo—school—schoolmaster ? Do you think he cares for him ? "

" Yes, it was he who sent him to the Agricultural School."

" The schoolmaster ? "

" The schoolmaster ! "

" Listen now Marit, I will not have any more of this nonsense, you must leave, you give me only sorrow and trouble, it was just the same with your mother, only sorrow and trouble.   I am an old man, and I wish to see you well provided for, and I will not be talked about as a fool in this matter ; it is your own good that I have at heart, you may be sure of that, Marit. I may soon be gone, and then you would stand there alone ; what would have become of your mother if it had not been for me ?   Come now, Marit, be a good girl, and listen to what I say, I seek only your own good."

" No, you don't."

" How ?   What do I seek then ? "

"To have your own way without any regard to mine."

"You have a will of your own, have you, you young sea-bird? You think you know your own good, do you, little fool? I shall let you taste the birch rod, so tall and big you are. Now listen Marit, let me speak a little kindly with you. You are not so bad at the bottom, but you are deluded. You must attend to what I say, I am old and experienced. I am not so well off as people think, a poor cageless bird could soon fly away with the little I have; your father dived hard into it. No, let us take care of ourselves in this world, it is not better worth. It is all very well for the schoolmaster to talk, for he has money himself, and the priest too, they can afford to preach; but with us, who must work for our living, it is quite a different thing. I am old, and have gone through much; I can tell you, love is nice enough to talk about, and may do very well for the clergy and such, but it

won't do for the peasantry, they must look at it
in another light.   First subsistence you see,
then religion, then a little schooling, then a little
love if it so falls in ; but I tell you it is no use
to begin with love and end with victuals.   What
have you to say now Marit ? "

" I don't know."

" You don't know ? "

" Yes, but I do."

" What then ? "

" Must I say ? "

" Yes, of course you must."

" I am bound up in this love."

He stood a moment amazed, then, remember-
ing the many similar conversations leading only
to the same end, he shook his head, turned his
back and went.

He vented his wrath on the men, abused the
girls, beat the great dog, and nearly frightened
the life out of a little hen that had strayed in
the field, but to Marit he said nothing.

That evening Marit was so happy when she went up stairs to bed, that she opened her window, looked out, and sang. She had got a fine little book from Ovind, and in it was a fine little love song,—this she sang :—

> Do you love me true,
> E'en as I love you,
> All the livelong happy day ;—
> The summer quickly flies,
> The leaf and blossom dies,
> But to come again we say.

> What you said before,
> Comes to me o'er and o'er,
> Like a small bird in a tree,—
> Flutters his tiny wings,
> Nestles himself and sings,
> Merrily chirping, happy and free.

> Litli, litli, lu,
> Do you hear me, you,
> Laddie from the birch hedge under?
> Darkness falleth fast,
> Daylight soon is past,
> Who's to guide me home I wonder !

> Garry, garry, giss,
> Sang I of a kiss ?
> Nay, my love, that ne'er can be,—
> Do you say you doubt it ?

Think no more about it,
I shall slip away you see.

Oh, goodnight, goodnight,
Dreamland seems so bright,
Whispering of your blue eyes true, —
Of the little silent word,
Once, you know, I overheard,
Oh, it was so rash of you !

See, I shut the door,
Do you want me more?
Echoes falling on mine ear,
Ticing and laughing free,
Do you want more with me?
The night is so mild and clear.

CHAP. XII.

THE OLD MAN GETS IIIS OWN WAY.

FEW years have passed since the last scene.

It is in the Autumn; the schoolmaster is coming towards Heidegaard; he opens the outside door, finds nobody at home, goes further in, still nobody there, till he comes to the innermost room;—there sits Ole Nordistuen in front of his bed, gazing at his hands.

The schoolmaster salutes him, and is welcomed; takes a stool, and seats himself in front of Ole.

" You have sent for me."

" Yes, I have."

The schoolmaster looks round, takes a book that is lying on the sofa and opens it.

" What was it you wanted with me ? "

" I am just thinking it over."

The schoolmaster takes his time, brings out his spectacles to read the title of the book, dries them, and puts them on.

" You are getting old now, Ole."

" Yes, it was just about that I wanted to see you ; things go wrong, and I shall soon be gone."

. " Then you should see that you are ready to go, Ole ; " he shuts the book, and sits looking at the binding.

" It's a good book you have in your hand, there."

" Yes, that's true;—have you often got beyond the fly leaf, Ole ? "

" Lately, yes—"

The schoolmaster lays the book aside, and puts his spectacles by.

"Things are not just as you would wish them now, Ole."

"Nor have they been as far back as I can remember."

"Well it was the same with me for a long time. I was not on good terms with a friend of mine, I wanted him to come to me, and I was miserable; at last I bethought me I would go to him, and since then I have been happy."

Ole looks up, but is silent.

The schoolmaster: "How do you think the farm is doing, Ole?"

"It is going backwards like myself."

"Who will take it when you are gone?"

"It is just this I don't know, and it troubles me."

"Your neighbours are doing well, Ole."

"Yes, they have the Agriculturist to help them."

The schoolmaster turns towards the window, saying somewhat carelessly, "You should have help too Ole, you can't walk much, and you know very little of the new method."

" Oh, there's no one who would help me !"

" Have you asked anyone ? "

But Ole makes no reply.

The schoolmaster: " It was long thus between myself and God. ' Thou art not good to me,' I said to Him. ' Hast thou asked me to be so?' He replied. No, I had not, then I prayed, and all things went on well. "

Ole is still silent, and now the schoolmaster is silent too.

At last Ole says, " I have a grandchild ; she knows what it would please me to see before I am borne away, but she does not do it."

The schoolmaster smiles : " Perhaps it would not please her ? There are many things that trouble you, but so far as I can see, all the difficulties centre at last on the farm."

Ole replies feelingly: " Yes, it has passed from

one generation to another, and the soil is good.
All that father after father has got together, has
been laid out there, and now things don't grow.
Neither do I know, when I am taken away, who
shall come in my stead.   He cannot be of our
kindred."

"But there is your granddaughter.—"

"But he who takes her, how will he manage
the farm?   This I long to know before I die.
There is haste Baard, both for me and the farm."

After a pause, the schoolmaster said, "Shall
we go out a little and look at the farm, this fine
day?"

"Yes, let us go, I have labourers up there; they
gather the leaves, but they don't work except
they see me."

He hobbled for his great cap and stick, saying
as he went, "They don't like working for me,
I don't know how it is."

"On coming out and turning the corner,
he exclaimed, "Here you see, no order; the

wood scattered all over, the axe not stuck in the log." He bent over with difficulty, took it up and slashed it in.

"There, do you see that sheep skin fallen down, but has any one hung it up?" He did it himself.

"And there is the ladder out of place." He put it right, and turning to the schoolmaster, said, "The same thing day after day!"

As they went further they heard a lively song from the fields.

"Hark! they are singing at work," said the schoolmaster.

"No, it is little Knut Ostistuen who is singing; he is gathering leaves for his father. It is over there my people are working, they are not singing."

"It is not one of the country songs, that?"

"No, I hear it is not."

"Ovind Pladsen has been a great deal in Ostistuen; it must be one of those he has introduced; where he is, there is sure to be song."

No reply.

The field they went over was not in good condition, it wanted attention. The schoolmaster remarked it, whereupon Ole stopped.

"I cannot do any more," ·he said, almost in tears; "but it is hard to go over such a field, you may be sure."

As they began to talk again about the size of the farm, and what most required attention, they concluded to go up the hill side, where they could overlook the whole. When they had reached the place, and could see the farm laid out before them, the old man was quite moved.

"I should not like to leave it as it is. We have worked hard there both I and my parents before me; but now nothing is to be seen of our labour."

Just then, right above their heads, there burst out a song, with that peculiar sharpness that a lad's voice has when it is changing. They were

not far from the tree where little Knut Ostistuen
was sitting, pulling leaves for his father, and
they listened to the song :—

> All along by copse and glade
>   Up the rocky mountain,
> Thro' the pleasant birch wood's shade,
>   By the silver fountain.
> Chase away each thought of care,
>   Gaily, gladly singing,
> Through the pure and bracing air
>   Joyful echoes ringing.
>
> The birds salute from every tree,
>   They form a charming choir,
> The air grows pure, and light, and free,
>   Higher up and higher.
> So the thought of childhood's hours
>   To the memory rushes,
> Recollections from the flowers
>   Peep with rosy blushes.
>
> Stay and listen ;—it is good,
>   To thy heart appealing—
> The grand deep song of solitude,
>   Speaks to every feeling.
> But a streamlet gurgling on,
>   But a small stone rolling,
> Calls up forgotten duties gone,
>   Like a death knell tolling.

Tremble, yes, but pray, poor soul
  'Midst thy saddest thinking ;—
Forward to the blesséd goal,—
  Keep thy heart from sinking.
There is Christ as once of old,
  Elias too, and Moses ;
When their glory ye behold,
  Faith in joy reposes.

Ole had seated himself, and hid his head in his hands.

"Let us talk together here," said the schoolmaster, and sat down by his side.

———

Down at the little farm, Ovind had just returned from a long journey, the chaise was still at the door, while the horses were resting.

Although Ovind had now a good salary as District Agriculturist, he still kept his little room, down at Pladsen, and assisted them in his spare time. Pladsen was now under good cultivation from one end to the other, but it was so small that Ovind called it "Mother's doll's play ;" for it was chiefly she who managed the farm.

He had just dressed after his journey, and so had the father who had come home white from the mill, and they were speaking of going out a little before supper, when the mother came in looking quite pale :

"Do look out, pray see the strangers coming to the house ! "

They both went to the window, and Ovind was the first to exclaim,—

"It is the schoolmaster, and,——yes, I do believe it is,——yes, it is him ! "

"Yes, it is old Ole Nordistuen," said Thore, as he turned from the window to avoid being seen, for they were close at hand.

Ovind got a glance from the schoolmaster, as he retreated from the window ; Baard smiled and looked back at old Ole, who was labouring along with his stick, and the small short steps, the one leg always lifted higher than the other. From inside they could hear the schoolmaster saying, " He has only just come home ;" and Ole to repeat twice, " Hm-hm."

They waited a long time in the passage, the mother had gone to the pantry where the milk stood, Ovind had his old place, his back leaning against the great table, his face to the door, and the father sat by his side. At last there came a knock, and in walked the schoolmaster, and took his hat off, then old Ole, and took his cap off, but back he turned to shut the door, and stood a long time, manifestly at a loss. Thore rose, and bade them be seated ; they sat side by side on the window sill. Thore sat down again.

Now thus was the matter settled.

The schoolmaster : " We have had beautiful weather this Autumn."

Thore : "Yes, it has taken up of late."

" It will be sure to last so long as the wind remains in the same quarter."

" Are you ready with the harvest up there ? "

"No, indeed, Ole Nordistuen here, as perhaps you know, would like to have your help, Ovind, if there's nothing in the way?"

Ovind : "When I am requested, I shall be glad to do what I can."

"Yes, but it wasn't only just for the present, he meant. He sees the farm is not doing well, and he thinks it is the right method and over-sight that are wanting."

Ovind : "I am so little at home."

The schoolmaster looks at Ole, who feels that it is his turn to speak now, he moves uneasily a few times, and then begins quickly and abruptly: "It was, it is,—yes,—I thought you might stay,—that is, you might live with us up there, be there, when you were not away on your journeys."

"I thank you very much for the offer, but I should prefer to stay where I am."

Ole looks at the schoolmaster, who explains:

"Things seem in a muddle for Ole to-day;

you see he was here once before, and the recollection of it makes it rather awkward."

Ole, quickly : "Yes, that's it, I went on like a fool, I was striving so long with the girl, that the edge of the axe grew blunt. But byegones shall be byegones. Rain brooks soon dry up. May snow does not last long. It is not thunder that kills people."

They all laughed, and the schoolmaster said, "Ole means that you must forget the past, and you also, Thore."

Ole looks, and does not know whether he dare begin again.

Then Thore says, "A sharp cut mends sooner than a tear, and you will find no scar upon me."

Ole: "I did not know the lad that time. Now I see that things prosper under his hand; Autumn answers to Spring ; he has money at his finger ends, and I should like to get hold of him."

Ovind looks at his father, and he at the

mother, she from them to the schoolmaster, and at last all eyes were fixed upon him.

"Ole means that he has a large farm—"

Ole interrupts: "A large farm but ill cultivated;—I cannot do more, I am old, and my feet refuse to obey my commands, but it would repay anyone to have a pull up there."

"The largest farm in the district, and no mistake!" says the schoolmaster.

"The largest farm in the district; that is just the misfortune, for great shoes won't keep on; it is all right to have a good gun, but you must be able to lift it." (With a quick glance at Ovind,) "You could perhaps give me a lift could you?"

"To manage the farm?"

"Just so; you should have the farm."

"Should I GET the farm?"

"Just so; and so you would have the charge of it."

"But?—"

" Will you not ? "

" Yes, of course."

" Yes yes, yes yes, then it is settled, said the hen, when she flew on to the water."

" But ?——"

Ole looks inquiringly at the schoolmaster.

"Ovind wants to know if he is to have Marit ? "

Ole quickly, " Marit into the bargain, Marit into the bargain ! "

Ovind jumped up and laughed for joy, rubbed his hands, and ran about, repeating continuously, " Marit into the bargain ! Marit into the bargain ! "

Thore laughed in deep chuckles ; the mother sat up in the corner, with eyes constantly fixed on her son, till the tears came.

Ole, very eagerly : " What do you think of the farm ?"

" It's excellent soil ! "

" Excellent, isn't it ? "

" And matchless pastures ! "

" Matchless pastures! Will it carry through?"

" It shall be the best farm in the district ! "

" The best farm in the district ?   Do you think so ?   Do you mean it ? "

" As true as I stand here."

" Just as I said ! "

They both of them spoke equally quickly, and corresponded to each other like a pair of wheels.

" But the money, you see, the money ?   I have no money."

" We shall get on slowly without money, but still we shall get on !"

" We shall get on !   To be sure we shall get on ! But things would improve much quicker if we HAD money you say ?"

" A very great deal quicker."

" A great deal ? We should have had money ; yes, yes ; but one can chew without all one's teeth ; he who drives only with oxen still gets on."

The mother stood and winked at Thore, who often glanced up quickly at her as he sat and rocked himself backwards and forwards, stroking his hands down over his knees; the schoolmaster blinked at him.

Thore cleared his throat a little, and tried to begin, but Ole and Ovind were talking so incessantly, laughing and making such a noise, that it was impossible for any one else to be heard.

"Could you be quiet a little, Thore has something to say," breaks in the schoolmaster, at which they stop and look at Thore.

At last he begins in a low tone, "It has happened that at this place we have had a mill, and of late years it has happened we have had two. From year to year we have always had a penny or two from these mills ; but neither my father nor I have touched the money, excepting that time Ovind was away. The schoolmaster had it in charge, and he says it has prospered,—

but now it is best that Ovind should get it for Nordistuen."

The mother stood in the corner, making herself quite little, as with a face glowing with pleasure she gazed at Thore, who, on his part, sat immoveable, and looking almost stupid ; Ole Nordistuen sat in front of him with gaping mouth ; Ovind was the first to recover himself from the surprise, and breaking out : " Good luck attends me !" went across the room to his father, clapped him on the shoulder. " Oh father ! " said he, rubbed his hands, and went back again.

" How much money will it be ?" Ole asked at last, speaking in a low tone to the schoolmaster.

" Oh, not so very little."

" A few hundred ? "

" More than that."

" More than that ? Ovind, more than that ! Good gracious, what a farm it will be !" He rose up and laughed aloud.

"I must go up with you to see Marit," said Ovind, "we'll take the chaise that is standing outside, and be quick there."

"Yes, quick, quick! Do you, then, want everything quick?"

"Yes, quick and rash."

"Quick and rash! Exactly as when I was young, exactly!"

"Here is your cap and stick, and now I'm going to turn you out!"

"You turn me out, ha, ha, ha! But you are coming with me, really, are you not? The others must come too; we must sit together to-night so long as there is a spark in the embers, come along!"

They promised. Ovind helped him up into the carriage, and they were off to Nordistuen. The great dog was not the only one up there that was astonished when Ole Nordistuen drove into the farmstead with Ovind Pladsen. Whilst Ovind was helping him out of the carriage, and

the servants and laborers were staring with open
mouths, Marit came out into the passage to see
what it was the dog was so incessantly barking
at ; but when she saw, she stopped as though
she were glued to the spot, then grew desperately
red, and ran in again. When old Ole got into
the room, however, he called out so terifically to
her, that she could do no other than come forth
again.

"Go and get ready, child, here is the one that
shall have the farm ! "

" Is it possible ? " she exclaims almost without
knowing it, and so loud that it rang again.

" Yes, it is possible ! " answers Ovind, clapping
his hands ; thereupon she swings round on one
foot, tosses that she has in her hand far away,
and runs out ; Ovind follows.

The schoolmaster soon came with Thore and
his wife ; the old man had got a lamp on the
table, which was decked with a white cloth ; he
called for wine and beer, and he, himself, went

M

busily round and round, lifting his legs even further up than usual, and still the right foot higher than the left.

Before this little story is concluded, it may be told that five weeks after, Ovind and Marit were married' in Sognet's church. The schoolmaster himself led the song that day, as the sexton was ill. His voice was broken, for he was old, but Ovind thought it did him good to hear him. And when he had given Marit his hand and led her up to the altar, the schoolmaster nodded to him from the choir, just like Ovind had pictured it, as he sat so depressed at that dance ; he nodded back again, while the tears would run down.

Those tears at the dance were the forerunners of these here, and between them lay his faith and his work.

Here ends the story of Ovind.

THE EAGLE'S NEST.

THE FATHER.

THE EAGLE'S NEST.

ENDREGAARDEN was the name of a small solitary hamlet, surrounded by high mountains, from which flowed a broad river that divided the flat and fertile valley in two.

The river ran into a lake that lay close to the hamlet, and from this spot there was a beautiful prospect. Once there came a man rowing over Endre Water ; his name was Endre, and it was he who had first settled in the valley, and his kindred who now lived there. Some said he had decamped hither for murder's sake, and it was therefore his descendants were so dark ; others said it was due to the mountains, that shut out the sun at five o'clock on midsummer day.

Over this hamlet there hung an eagle's nest from the projecting cliffs up in the mountain, and though all could see when the eagle was sitting, the nest was quite out of reach. The male bird sailed over the hamlet, pouncing now on a lamb, now on a kid, once he had also taken a little child and borne away; therefore there was no security so long as the eagle had her nest in this mountain fastness.

There was a tradition among the people, that in the olden time, two brothers had climbed up and destroyed the nest; but now there was no one who could do it.

When two met in Endregaarden, they would speak of the eagle's nest, and look up. Every one knew what time in the new year the eagles had come back, where they had pounced down and done mischief, and who had last attempted to climb up.

In the hope of one day being able to achieve the feat of the two brothers, the lads, from quite small boys, would practise themselves in climbing trees and cliffs, wrestling, &c.

At the time of which we now speak, the first lad in Endregaarden was not of the Endre kin ; his name was Leif, he had curly hair, and small eyes, was clever in all play, and fond of the gentler sex. He said very early of himself, that one day he would reach the eagle's nest, but people intimated he had better not have said it aloud.

This tickled him, and before he was of full age, he went aloft. It was a clear Sunday morning in the early summer; the young birds would scarcely be hatched. The people gathered in a crowd under the mountain to see; old and young alike advising him against the attempt.

But he listened only to the voice of his own strong will, and waiting till the eagle left her nest, he made one spring and hung in a tree several yards from the ground. It grew in a cleft, and up this cleft he began to climb. Small stones loosened from under his feet, and the soil and gravel came tumbling down, otherwise it was quite still, save the sound of the river from behind with its subdued and ceaseless sough.

He soon reached that part where the mountain began to project, and here he hung by one hand, groping with his foot for a hold; he could not see. Many, especially women, turned away, saying he would not have done this if his parents had been living. At last he found a footing, sought again, first with the hand, then with the foot; he missed, slipped, then hung fast again. They who stood below could hear each other breathing.

Then a tall young girl, who sat upon a stone apart from the rest, rose up; they said she had promised herself to him from a child, although he was not of the Endre kin, and her parents would never give their consent. She stretched out her arms and called aloud, "Leif, Leif, why do you do this!" Every one turned towards her; the father stood close by and gave her a severe look, but she did not heed him. "Come down again, Leif," she cried: "I, I love you, and there's nothing to be gained up there!"

One could see that he was considering, he waited a moment or two, and then went further up. He found a firm footing, and for a time he got on well; then he seemed to grow tired, for he often stopped.

A small stone came rolling down, as though it were a forerunner, and all who stood there must watch its course to the bottom. Some could not bear it longer, and went away. The girl still standing high upon the stone, wrung her hands and gazed up. Leif took hold again with one hand; it slipped, she saw it distinctly; he made a grasp with the other, it slipped also;

"Leif!" she cried, so that it rang in the mountain, and all the others joined in. "He's slipping!" they cried, and stretched out their hands towards him, men and women. He continued to slip with the sand, stone, and soil; slip, slip, faster, faster. The people turned away, and then they heard a rustling and rattling on the mountain behind them, and something heavy fall down like a great piece of wet earth. When they looked round again, there he lay, torn and disfigured. The girl lay on the stone; the father took her up and carried her away.

The lads, who had the most excited Leif to climb, dared not now go near to help him, some could not even look at him; so the old people had to come forward. The eldest of them said, as he took him up, "Alas! alas! but,—" he added, "it is well there is something hangs so high that every one cannot reach it."

FINIS.

THE FATHER.

HORD OVERAAS, of whom we are about to speak, was the wealthiest man in the parish.

His tall figure stood one day in the pastor's study: "I have got a son," he said eagerly, "and I wish to have him baptised."

"What shall he be called?"

"Finn, after my father."

"And his god parents?"

They were named, being relatives of Thord, and the best men and women in the district.

"Is there anything else?" asked the pastor, and looked up.

The farmer stood a minute ;

" I should like to have him baptised by him-self," he said.

" That is to say on a week day ? "

" Next Saturday, at twelve o'clock."

" Is there anything else ? "

" Nothing else."

The farmer took his hat, and moved to go.

Then the pastor rose ; " There is still this," he said, and going up to Thord, he took his hand, and looked him in the face : " God grant that the child may be a blessing to you ! "

Sixteen years after that day, Thord stood again in the pastor's study.

" You look exceedingly well, Thord," said the pastor ; he saw no change in him.

" I have no trouble," replied Thord.

" The pastor was silent, but a moment after : " What is your errand to-night ? " he asked.

" I have come to-night about my son, who is to be confirmed to-morrow."

" He is a clever lad."

" I did not wish to pay the pastor, before I heard what number he would get."

" I hear that,—and here are ten dollars for the pastor."

" Is there anything else ? " asked the pastor, he looked at Thord.

" Nothing else." Thord went.

Eight years more passed by, and so one day the pastor heard a noise without his door, for many men were there, and Thord first among them. The pastor looked up and recognised him: " You come with a powerful escort to-night."

I have come to request that the banns may be published for my son ; he is to be married to Karen Storliden, daughter of Gudmund, who is here with me."

" That is to say, to the richest girl in the parish."

" They say so, replied the farmer, he stroked his hair up with one hand.

The pastor sat a minute as in thought, he said nothing, but entered the names in his books, and the men wrote under.

Thord laid three dollars on the table.

" I should have only one," said the pastor.

" Know that perfectly, but he is my only child ; will do the thing well."

The pastor took up the money : " This is the third time now, Thord, that you stand here on your son's account."

" But now I am done with him," said Thord, took up his pocket book, said good night, and went. The men slowly followed.

Just a fortnight after this, the father and son were rowing over the lake in still weather to Storliden, to arrange about the wedding.

" The cushion is not straight," said the son, he rose up to put it right. At the same moment his foot slipped ; he stretched out his arms, and with a cry fell into the water.

" Catch hold of the oar ! " called the father,

he stood up and stuck it out. But when the son had made a few attempts, he became stiff.

"Wait a minute!" cried the father, and began to row. Then the son turned backwards over, gazed earnestly at his father, and sank.

Thord could scarcely believe it to be true; he kept the boat still, and stared at the spot where his son had sunk, as though he would come up again. A few bubbles rose up, a few more, then one great one, it burst—and the sea again lay bright as a mirror.

For three days and three nights the father was seen to row round and round the spot without either food or sleep; he was seeking for his son. On the morning of the third day he found him, and carried him up over the hills to his farm.

It would be about a year after that day, when the pastor, one autumn evening, heard something rustling outside the door in the passage, and fumbling about the lock. The door opened, and in walked a tall thin man, with bent figure and white hair. The pastor looked long at him before he recognised him ; it was Thord.

"Do you come so late?" asked the pastor and stood still before him.

"Why yes, I do come late," said Thore, he seated himself. The pastor sat down also, as though waiting ; there was a long silence.

Then said Thord, "I have something with me that I wish to give to the poor,"—he rose, laid some money on the table, and sat down again.

The pastor counted it : "It is a great deal of money," he said.

"It is the half of my farm, which I have sold to-day."

The pastor remained long sitting in silence ; at last he asked, but gently : "What do you intend to do now?"

"Something better."

They sat there awhile, Thord with downcast

eyes, the pastor with his raised to Thord. Then the pastor said slowly, and in a low tone : " I think at last your son has really become a blessing to you."

" Yes, I think so myself also," said Thord, he looked up, and two tears coursed slowly down his face.

BURNETT AND HOOD, MIDDLESBROUGH.